HOT CHOCOLATE AND A FESTIVE FATALITY

A WATERWHEEL CAFE MYSTERY

VICTORIA TAIT

KANGA
PRESS

DEDICATION

To Irene Soulsby, Amber, and Jessica
Thank you for your support and for backing my Kickstarter
campaign, which made this book possible.

CHAPTER ONE

"Do you think we'll have a white Christmas?" Zivah asked.

"It feels cold enough, but I'm not sure I really want one," replied thirty-four-year-old Keya Varma as she walked beside her younger sister, who was pushing a compact black buggy. Zivah's baby son, Kaami, gurgled contentedly inside the buggy, snug in his padded brown fleece onesie, complete with little reindeer antlers.

"Why?" asked Zivah, a note of surprise in her voice. "You're usually so excited about Christmas. I know the broken boiler and burst pipe in your house has upset you, but I love having you around, and you can stay with us as long as you like."

Keya smiled gratefully at her sister. She did enjoy their time together, and it was fun preparing meals and sitting down to eat as a family, but she missed her little house in the small Cotswold village of Ampney St Martin.

Zivah lived with her husband, Aadi, in Stratton, a village on the northerly edge of Cirencester, which had been absorbed by the expanding market town.

Keya sighed. "I guess I'm ready for the year to end, so I can start afresh in January. And I'm not sure what to do about my police work after my sick leave finishes. I miss my colleagues, and solving cases is satisfying, but these last few months I've enjoyed running the cafe. We bring people real joy. That woman's face was a picture yesterday when she tried one of Mick's Christmas chocolate, cranberry and macadamia brownies. I was bursting with pride."

Keya finally smiled and as she did, the grey clouds parted, and a shaft of weak sunlight fell on the footpath ahead of them.

"Hi!" called a familiar voice.

Keya looked up and saw the tall figure and boyish face of recently promoted Sergeant Ryan Jenkins on the other side of Limes Lane. He was an enthusiastic and tech-savvy police colleague at Cirencester Station.

Keya and Zivah crossed the quiet road and approached a bungalow. They found Ryan, wearing jeans and a padded jacket, standing outside the bungalow beside an old table. A tall, thin, white-haired man, wearing an old tweed flat cap, was with him.

"Making the most of the dry weather," remarked the elderly man as he peered into the buggy.

Kaami smiled back at him.

"He's growing," commented the man.

"Thankfully. He's finally keeping some food down," Zivah replied. "Have you met my sister, Keya?"

"No, Larry Shipton. You're a colleague of Ryan's, aren't you?" the elderly man asked.

"I am." Keya smiled warmly back at Larry.

"But it's a rum business," muttered Larry.

Ryan's eyes widened.

"What is?" Keya asked.

Confused, Larry looked up at the considerably taller and much younger Ryan.

Ryan sighed. "The inspector said we weren't to worry you while you're on sick leave, but I suppose you should know that the chief constable sent a team to review Cirencester station. They've been poking around for the last month."

"I remember when they closed thirteen police stations," mused Larry, shaking his head. "Cost-cutting and efficiency, they said. But I called it a lack of community support and policing."

"There you go, sis," said Zivah, turning to Keya. "Take the redundancy package and concentrate on your cafe."

It sounded simple. But suddenly, Keya wasn't so certain she wanted to walk away from her police work and more than fifteen years in the Gloucestershire constabulary, despite what she'd said earlier about enjoying her time running the cafe.

Zivah turned back to Larry and Ryan and asked, "What are you doing?"

"Making improvements to my stall," replied Larry cheerfully.

Glancing down the drive at the side of Larry's bungalow, Keya wondered if he intended to sell what looked like an old fridge, a bike wheel, and other bits and pieces which were lying around.

"Gerald Sadler's Christmas light display is attracting visitors who park outside Larry's property …" Ryan began.

"So I thought I'd try selling them some of my winter veg, and my honey and jams," Larry explained.

Which was very enterprising, Keya thought.

"You won't be standing out here in the cold all evening, will you?" Zivah asked, sounding concerned.

"Nah," laughed Larry. "I'll just leave an honesty box for folks to use, and bring everything in before I go to bed, so the frost doesn't get to 'em."

"Is the festive light display really that spectacular?" asked Keya.

"It's certainly bright," Ryan replied, "But cheerful too. I have a great view from my bedroom window."

Ryan pointed to a pair of semi-detached Cotswold stone cottages located beyond Larry's property, set back from Limes Lane. They belonged to the farm at the end of the road, and Ryan had moved into one of them during the summer.

"I'm not sure what my Janet would have thought," commented Larry. "Over fifty years living opposite a paddock and feeding apples to the various ponies which grazed there. But she's gone, God rest her soul, and so are the ponies, and we have three brand new houses. They call it progress," Larry remarked in a voice which made it clear he disagreed.

"What are the new residents like?" Keya asked. "Wasn't there some trouble earlier in the year?"

"That was me," Larry replied proudly, standing a little taller. "The pushy developer was trying to bully me out of my house, but Ryan put a stop to it, didn't you, lad? Now hold that plank steady," he instructed Ryan.

Ryan held a piece of wood upright against the side of the table and Larry leaned down, put a nail against the wood, and hit it hard with a hammer.

Whack.

After several more hits, the nail penetrated the plank and when Ryan let go, it stood firm.

"Oy! Would you stop makin' such a racket? It's Sunday morning and some of us are tryin' to get a bit of peace and quiet!" shouted a man with a loud Irish voice which was more likely to disturb his neighbours than Larry's brief hammering.

"Ay, and others are trying to work," muttered Larry.

Keya considered the young man standing in the open doorway of the first of the three new executive houses. He was wearing a pair of pull-up trousers and a white T-shirt which, even from this distance, accentuated his muscled torso. A gold necklace glinted at his neck.

"That's Jackson Kelly," whispered Zivah. "He's caused a few issues with his neighbours since moving in, hosting wild parties and playing loud music."

Keya heard a deep bark, and a large, muscular Treeing Walker Coonhound trotted down the drive of the new house just as the first car she'd seen since leaving Zivah's house drove steadily along Limes Lane.

Without thinking, Keya dashed into the road, grabbing the large dog by the collar and pulling him back onto the pavement as a shocked-looking vicar braked sharply to a halt.

"Jackson!" exclaimed a female voice with a trace of a European accent. "What have I said about leaving the door open?"

Keya watched as a young woman with long blonde hair, wearing a skimpy, cropped pink satin camisole and matching shorts, pushed past the man.

The vicar drove on as the woman tottered down her drive and across the road wearing a pair of wedge slippers with pink fluffy straps across the front.

"Close your mouth lad," warned Larry, as Ryan stared at the new arrival.

"Chief," exclaimed the woman. "Thank you. I don't know how many times I've told Jackson to keep the front door shut. I'm Gabrielle, by the way."

"Nice to meet you, and I suggest you install a gate across your drive to prevent future accidents," Keya said.

Momentarily disappointed, Gabrielle nodded and replied, "Of course. I told Jackson the same thing, but he's done nothing about it. Perhaps I could pay you two to do it for me." She looked enquiringly at Larry and Ryan.

Ryan appeared tongue-tied, so Larry replied, "Ay, we can help you with that, lass."

Gabrielle gave Larry a dazzling smile before turning and swaying back across the road with Chief trotting beside her, his tail wagging as he followed.

Beside Keya, Zivah laughed quietly, and when Gabrielle was safely back inside her house, she remarked, "I don't think Gabrielle was happy that you didn't recognise her, sis."

Looking enquiringly at her sister, Keya asked, "Should I have done?"

"She's something on the internet," announced Larry.

"Haven't you seen the Christmas advert on TV for Chic Boutique? She's one of the models," Zivah explained.

"Oh," replied Keya, glancing back at the large house with an illuminated Christmas wreath on the door and a snowman beside it.

Larry considered, "Maybe there are some upsides to having new neighbours."

CHAPTER TWO

Keya and Zivah said their goodbyes to Ryan and Larry Shipton, crossed the road and manoeuvred Kaami's buggy onto the pavement running in front of the three new houses on Limes Lane.

As they did, the bells of the church beside the last house started ringing.

Keya wondered what Jackson, who lived in the first house, thought of the new noise on the otherwise quiet street.

Whack. Larry hammered a nail into another piece of wood.

Keya noticed a ladder placed against the side of the second house. A grey-haired man wearing glasses stepped out of the front door, manhandling a large, inflated Father Christmas.

He crossed to the ladder and began climbing it, with Santa slung across his shoulder.

Concerned for the man's safety, Keya and Zivah stopped to watch.

"Do you need any help?" Keya called.

The man froze, looked across at her, and frowned. "No, I can manage," he replied in a dismissive tone.

"He could at least be polite," Zivah whispered, as a woman wearing a fleece dressing gown tied around her ample waist stepped out of the front door and looked across at the figure on the ladder.

"You be careful, Gerald,"

"Stop nagging, woman," Gerald called back in an irritated voice.

The woman looked at Zivah and Keya and shrugged. As she walked down the garden path towards them, she shook her head and said, "These lights will be the death of him. But how are you and baby Kaami?"

"We're both well, thank you, Glenda. And can I introduce my sister, Keya, who's staying with us for a while? Her boiler broke down and flooded her kitchen and living room."

"You poor thing." Glenda gave Keya a sympathetic smile. "But I bet it's nice living with Zivah and chatting about this and that. She's been so kind to me since we moved in, bringing lovely cakes round. Oh!" Glenda's hand shot to her mouth.

"You run the Waterwheel Café, don't you? I've suggested to Gerald that we should visit but… you know what men are like? Annie, from next door, said she'd go with me one day. She said you serve wonderful afternoon teas."

"We do, and you should come and try our special festive tea," Keya replied enthusiastically. "My chefs have worked really hard putting the menu together and trying out different recipes. I can't wait to see what they're going to serve."

"Oh, it's a surprise to you, too. How exciting." Glenda looked wistfully at Keya.

"Glenda!" shouted Gerald. "Stop gossiping and hand me those lights."

Glenda gave Keya and Zivah a final smile and said, "I better go. He'll only natter at me if I don't help."

Keya and Zivah had only walked a few steps when the front door of the third house opened and a smartly dressed couple stepped out.

The woman, who was small and very thin, stopped to adjust a plant in a pretty container of brightly coloured flowers beside the front door.

"Don't do that," admonished her overweight husband who was wearing a charcoal grey suit. "Your hands will be covered in soil, and how will that look when we're introduced to Lord and Lady Bathurst?"

A silver Volvo SUV pulled up on the opposite side of the road as the well-dressed man strode down his garden path, his wife following more slowly.

As she closed the garden gate, a lady climbed out of the Volvo and called in an upper-class voice, "Morning, Annie. Lovely flowers."

Annie beamed, but her husband scowled and grabbed her arm, pulling her away.

The woman from the Volvo and her younger companion crossed the road, but when she saw Keya, she halted, and then, as if she recalled Keya's name, she said, "Good morning, Sergeant Varma."

"Ma'am," Keya responded politely and let the two women walk ahead.

When the women had turned and entered the church through the wooden roofed-gateway, Zivah asked, "Who was that?"

"The chief constable's wife."

Zivah raised her eyebrows as she pushed Kaami's buggy forward.

After the church, the paved road came to an end and a narrow, muddy track continued between fields leading to a wood. This was Keya and Zivah's destination, as Keya wanted to see if there was any holly she could cut to decorate her Waterwheel Café.

"Gerald must have a lot of patience and dedication to decorate his house with so many festive lights," Keya considered.

"He's retired, and Glenda said it's become his obsession. He started simply at their old place, but each year his scenes become more elaborate."

"I can't help thinking he's lost the essence of Christmas. I know we're not Christians, but I like Amma's surprisingly liberal view of Jesus."

Their mother, Chandra Varma, who they affectionately called Amma, tended to see the world in black-and-white terms, and all things Indian were definitively on the correct side.

"That he's another aspect of God and that Christmas provides an opportunity to celebrate and thank him for the year that is coming to an end?" said Zivah.

"Exactly," Keya confirmed as the track narrowed further and they entered the wood.

"The vicar – the one who nearly ran Gabrielle's dog over earlier – has asked me to bring Kaami to the family service on Christmas morning. Would you like to join us?" Zivah asked.

"It would certainly make the day feel more special, especially if there are lots of excited children. But what about Aadi?" Keya asked, thinking of Zivah's husband.

"He said he'd prefer to stay at home and start cooking while I take Kaami. I'm glad Sujin's joining us for lunch. Would he like to come to church?"

"I'm not sure. I'll ask him. And yes, I'm glad he's coming too. He was brought up a Christian, so I'm chuffed he's spending Christmas Day with us, a Hindu family."

Zivah smiled at Keya and said, "That's quite a milestone in your relationship."

"It is," Keya agreed, feeling a warmth spread through her body. She and Sujin had been together formally for less than six months, but it was a relationship that felt natural, without the need to either impress or fight for each other's attention.

"Which is why I'm secretly hoping Amma and Appa won't come over. Is that an awful thing to say?"

"No, Amma can be full on, but she likes Sujin, so I wouldn't worry if they do come. And look, isn't that a holly bush?"

Most of the trees around them were bare and leafless, but just off the path was a green holly bush with dark, spiky leaves.

"Do you want to hold or cut?" asked Keya. Although her left arm had improved hugely since it had been paralysed in the summer, she still didn't have the strength to perform certain tasks.

"I'll hold it and then you can cut where you want to," suggested Zivah.

Keya took out a pocketknife and, with Zivah's help, cut several sprigs of holly. Some even had plump red berries on them.

Gathering up the cuttings, they placed them under the sleeping Kaami's buggy and turned around to walk back to Zivah's house.

As they left the shelter of the wood, Keya pulled her coat tightly around her as she was hit by a gust of cold air.

She said to Zivah, "I'm looking forward to your warm house and a nice cup of tea."

CHAPTER THREE

On Tuesday morning, Keya arrived bright and early at Akemans auction house and antique centre, where her café was situated, outside the Cotswold village of Coln Akeman.

Parking her metallic reef-blue VW Polo at the front of the gravel car park, she looked up at the three-storey converted mill building and wondered if she should suggest to Gilly Wimsey, who ran the antique centre housed within it, that they decorate the frontage and hang some festive lighting.

On a dull grey morning like today, it would provide a more cheerful welcome. Many cafés in the area closed during the winter months because of the dwindling number of tourists. But Keya had been surprised by how many people had visited her Waterwheel Café the previous winter, and that number only appeared to be increasing this year.

She unlocked the antique centre's heavy oak front door and carried inside the basket containing tins full of frangipane mince pies, which she'd made the previous day.

Despite pressure to open every day, Keya had resisted, and the café remained closed on Mondays. It gave her staff a break and allowed her to bake, cook, and consider new ideas for the café's menu.

Over her left shoulder, she was carrying another bag holding two pork and chicken terrines with apricots and pistachios, which she was planning to trial as a lunchtime special.

She switched on the lights and stepped into the large internal space which housed rows of the antique centre stalls and booths. It was eerie, and she waited for the lights to fully illuminate before closing the wooden door behind her and walking between two rows of stalls.

She passed one which held an eclectic mix of tables and displays of lamps with cream, white, or floral lampshades. A collection of curved-handle wooden walking sticks was displayed in a painted barrel container. On the other side, an old-fashioned wooden spinning wheel stood next to a basket of dried flowers presented in bunches in conical paper packages.

A few of the stalls had already hung colourful Christmas decorations and strands of unlit fairy lights, but overall, the centre did not feel festive. And neither did the café when she went in through a door at the rear of the antique centre.

Gilly, whose family owned the building, had designed the internal décor, which honoured the industrial heritage of the building.

The walls were either plain brick or painted cream, and the metal domed pendant lights hanging from the ceiling slowly came to life as Keya looked around her café. That was better, but she still felt the space needed sprucing up for Christmas.

On the return trip to her car to collect the holly she and Zivah had gathered, she met Mick Gospel, one of her chefs. He always reminded her of a professor with wispy brown hair, tinged with silver, and a pair of large, round, thin metal-framed glasses, until she remembered his arms, which were covered in tattoos from the time he'd spent in prison.

He was quiet, diligent, and hard-working, and had formed a strong bond with Monica, Ryan's mum, who also worked in the kitchen. Their quiet efficiency was a far cry from when Keya's own mother had cooked at the café, often helped by Gilly's bubbly Aunt Beanie.

"Can I help?" asked Mick, who was always conscious of Keya's disability and the lack of strength in her left arm.

But it was improving, she told herself.

Mick settled a small daypack on his back, picked up a bulky-looking shopping bag, and then took one of the bags of prickly holly from Keya.

Noticing the holly, Mick asked, "Are we putting up Christmas decorations? And what about a tree? I love a nice Christmas tree."

"We do need to do something," Keya agreed. "I'll speak to Gilly. What have you been baking?"

"Gingerbread shapes. Stars, men, and miniature houses. I had lots of fun icing and decorating them," replied Mick, smiling self-consciously.

"Are you still living on the edge of Cirencester?" asked Keya.

"Yes, behind Tesco's supermarket. I'd love to move somewhere quieter, but everything I've looked at has been too expensive."

"And what about travelling? Didn't Monica's safari trip to Africa reignite your interest in seeing the world?"

"Oh, she had such a wonderful time. I loved seeing her photos of all the animals, but that's also expensive. I'm going to sit down between Christmas and New Year, when we're closed, and see where I'd like to go and what is available.

Despite being open for the winter, she and her staff had agreed that they would need a break, and closing between Christmas and New Year seemed a sensible option.

Back in the café, Keya and Mick unpacked their baking, and Keya placed the terrines in a fridge. She would need to cut them into appropriately sized slices later.

At half past eight, when Monica had arrived, she, Mick, and Keya sat down with cups of tea and coffee to discuss the festive December menu.

"Would you like to join us?" Keya called across to Millie, who had the front-of-house role for the café. She was also Ryan's girlfriend.

Millie put down her cloth and plastic bottle of disinfectant spray and joined the others at the round wooden table. She removed the band from her ponytail, allowing her long blonde hair to fall around her shoulders.

"This is the first full week in December and Mick has already pointed out that the café doesn't feel very festive. I'll discuss decorations with Gilly when I next see her."

"And a tree?" Mick enquired again.

"And a Christmas tree," agreed Keya, jotting it down in her notebook. A habit she'd borrowed from her police work.

"Mick's baking reminded me of some adorable gingerbread men decorations I saw for the tree," Monica said, "and some red and white candy canes." She tucked a strand of her bobbed grey hair behind her ear.

"Oh, yes, food-themed decorations. I like that." Keya was starting to feel more enthusiastic about decorating the café.

"I think we should stick to natural decorations," Millie suggested. "Paper streamers and paper chains, or bunting made from cotton or hessian."

"Hessian?" Monica queried.

"Yes, like the brown sacks flour used to come in, or so I understand. I saw some great ones on Etsy which would be perfect for the feel of our café. And wooden and paper decorations."

"I like the sound of those," agreed Keya. "What about the menu? I made a couple of chicken and pork terrines to offer with salads as specials."

"We should order some bread to go with them from the Stone Circle Bakery," suggested Monica.

"Good idea." Keya made another note.

Monica continued, "And we have several soups to offer, don't we, Mick?"

"Er, yes. I found an interesting recipe for celeriac with hazelnuts and truffles, which I'd like to try.

"As long as the ingredients aren't too expensive," warned Keya.

"Point taken," Mick accepted. "And we could also make some sweet potato with ginger, which is always popular when it's cold. And how about a traditional French onion soup?"

"Served with slices of bread with melted cheese on top. Yummy!" Millie declared.

"They all sound great," agreed Keya. "And any suggestions for festive sandwich fillings?"

"Roast turkey with stuffing, and toasted Camembert cheese topped with cranberry sauce," suggested Monica.

"Ooh," sounded Millie. Then she apologised. "Sorry, I don't know why I have a thing for melted cheese at the moment. But it might be because Ryan and I tried a new Swiss restaurant in Cheltenham last Thursday."

"Before the pantomime?" Monica enquired.

"Yes, and it was such fun. I haven't been to one since I was a child."

As Millie was only in her early twenties, Keya didn't think it was that long ago.

"I'm not sure I've ever been to a pantomime. Well, not a proper one. I don't think prison productions count," Mick remarked. "What was it about?"

"Mother Goose, and they even showed a film of the goose running around Cheltenham causing mayhem," laughed Millie.

"That sounds wonderful," Mick said wistfully.

Keya made a mental note to suggest to Dotty that they invite Mick if she did organise a pantomime trip. Then she wrote it in her notebook to be sure she didn't forget.

"And I thought we could offer pigs in blankets as an extra hot sandwich," suggested Monica. "It has a festive ring to it, but all we need to do is wrap bacon around the sausages when we serve it."

"Excellent idea," Keya agreed, and wrote another note.

"Mick and I still need to finalise our thoughts on the festive afternoon tea menu we're going to offer from Thursday. Can we prepare some samples for you to try later?" Monica asked.

"Of course," Keya replied, as the door opened and one of the stallholders from the antique centre poked his head around and called, "Are you open? I'd love a cup of coffee and a bacon sandwich."

CHAPTER FOUR

A steady stream of visitors to the café kept Keya and her team busy for the rest of Tuesday morning, through lunchtime, and into the afternoon.

Alison, who lived nearby in Coln Akeman, helped serve, and Zivah arrived mid-morning after dropping Kaami at nursery and running some errands.

Keya was enjoying a bowl of tomato and basil soup when the café door opened, and her boss at Cirencester Police Station, Inspector Evans, walked in.

He was dressed in his habitual brown suit, which Keya thought was hanging a little more loosely than it used to on his burly, rugby-player frame.

His mother had died earlier in the year, and, despite his gruff manner and dismissal of any enquiry into his well-being, Keya did wonder how much her passing had affected him.

"Sergeant!" boomed the inspector in his deep baritone Welsh voice.

He was followed into the café by Ryan, wearing his police uniform, and retired police sergeant Stan Rowbottom, who now worked at the station in a civilian capacity, organising the filing and working for Inspector Evans in an unofficial capacity.

Keya wondered whether, if she wasn't passed fit enough to return to work, she might be offered a similar role.

"Can we join you?" asked the inspector, who was already pulling out a chair. He sat down opposite Keya, with Ryan and Stan on the other sides of the square table.

"That smells good," said Stan, sniffing the air.

"I'm afraid it's the last of this batch of soup, but Mick has prepared some new flavours with a festive feel."

"And that's not all he's helped prepare, is it, Sergeant Jenkins?" said the inspector, turning to Ryan.

Ryan blushed.

Keya frowned.

"Afternoon tea," stated the inspector. "We heard there was a tasting session and, as the station is quiet, we thought we'd volunteer."

Ryan shrugged his shoulders as Monica left the kitchen and walked towards the table.

"I see you've brought everyone," Monica said brightly.

"Stan and I aren't ones to miss an opportunity like this, and I do like your afternoon teas," the inspector said, grinning.

Glancing at Keya, Monica said, "Just remember, Keya has the final say."

Keya finished her soup and then cleared her throat. "Let's just see." She wasn't sure she could overrule the inspector as it wasn't something she was used to doing. "But first, tea?"

Stan and Inspector Evans nodded.

"Can I have a cappuccino?" Ryan asked.

Monica smiled indulgently at her son and, as she picked up Keya's empty bowl, she said, "I'm sure you can. Now, let me organise the food."

"And I'll sort out the drinks." Keya approached the drinks counter, behind which the barista, and former porter at the antique centre, Norman Climpson, checked his phone. It was unlike him to use it while working.

Norman looked up, frowning.

"Is everything OK?" Keya asked.

"I'm not sure. The council planning committee was making its decision today on converting the barn and changing its use to an antiques shop for Dotty. Beanie went to the meeting, and she's just messaged to say she's on her way here."

By Beanie, he was referring to Gilly's aunt. Norman lived with Aunt Beanie at Meadowbank Farm on the edge of Fairford, a small, local town. Keya's friend Dotty lived in a cottage adjacent to the main farmhouse, and she was planning to open an antiques shop in one of the farm's old barns.

Millie carried the cups, saucers, and milk and sugar. Once Norman had filled the teapot, Keya took it back to the table, where her police colleagues were muttering quietly amongst themselves. They fell silent as she set the teapot down.

Why did she have a feeling they were hiding something from her? But before she had a chance to confront them, Mick and Monica appeared, carrying three-tiered cake stands, which they placed on the table.

Monica waited for Keya to collect Ryan's cappuccino and sit down before she said, "We've provided each of you with a selection of sandwiches, savoury bites, cakes, and bakes. We've already agreed – if Keya is OK with it –" Monica glanced at Keya, "to serve a Christmas spiced fruit scone with cream and jam, which isn't part of today's selection."

Ryan looked disappointed, but Keya could understand why the scone had been left out. There were so many other inviting treats to sample.

"Here is a menu, and we'd appreciate it if you could score each item out of ten and add any additional comments." Monica handed each of them a paper menu and a pencil.

Keya sat back, sipped her tea, and watched with delight as her three colleagues tucked into their food.

Ryan was methodical and took the tasting seriously, lining up the six finger sandwiches, each with a different filling. He tasted them, one at a time, before writing a score on his menu.

Keya, being a vegetarian, had less choice of sandwiches, but she happily bit into an egg mayonnaise one ... with a hint of turmeric. It worked well with the sharpness of mustard.

"What's this?" Ryan asked. He'd finished his sandwiches and had now placed the savoury delicacies on his plate. Between his finger and thumb, he held what Keya recognised as a prune wrapped in bacon. Usually served hot as a Christmas canapé, it was an interesting option for the festive afternoon tea.

"That's what they call a devil on horseback," Inspector Evans proclaimed.

"Yes, but what is it?" queried Ryan.

"Just try it," said Stan, who lifted one off his stand and popped it in his mouth. When he finished chewing, he considered, "I like that, but I'm not sure it should be served cold."

"It's tasty," Ryan agreed. "But I'm still not sure what it was."

"A prune, lad. Keeps you regular," declared the inspector.

Ryan looked down at his plate uncertainly.

They continued eating, and Keya particularly enjoyed a brie and cranberry tart.

As they started on the cakes, Inspector Evans cleared his throat and said, "Sergeant Jenkins told me he let slip that the station is under review, so I thought it was time we levelled with you."

Ryan blushed again as he bit into a square of cherry and pistachio Battenberg cake.

The inspector continued, "It wasn't a surprise to the chief inspector, or to me, when the review team arrived, as there have been mutterings about efficiency and specialist teams in Gloucestershire for a while. We've done well to continue as we are, probably because our case clear-up rate is high, but the writing is on the wall."

"Which means what?" Keya asked as she bit into a crisp French macaron with a rich buttercream filling.

The menu said it was flavoured with prosecco and elderflower. She could certainly taste the elderflower. It felt surreal to be sampling such delicacies while discussing the future of their jobs.

"We're unlikely to hear anything formally until Christmas, or the New Year, but some departments are likely to close. And I suspect our team is top of the list. The murder team at headquarters has been grumbling about us for a while. I'd say they're jealous and want us incorporated into their team."

Keya allowed the news to sink in as she chewed her macaron. It wasn't entirely unexpected.

It had been clear when a temporary replacement for Inspector Evans had run their team, while he'd been on compassionate leave caring for his dying mother, that their practices, while effective, were not in line with modern police policies and procedures.

But she couldn't help feeling sad, and that the change wouldn't benefit the local Cotswold residents. There was only one dedicated rural engagement officer. The position had been hers, but in her absence, Ryan had taken it over. Moving the serious crimes team away to Gloucester would further isolate the rural community.

"So who will be left in Cirencester?" Keya asked.

"That's what we're waiting to find out," said the inspector levelly.

Keya gasped. "They won't close the station, will they?" She stared at Inspector Evans, her eyes wide with concern.

"It is a possibility, although I know Chief Inspector Greg has spent a lot of time over the past few months lobbying for its retention."

Keya was pleased to hear this and hoped that, as he'd previously worked at headquarters, his concerns would be listened to.

"So what do we do?" asked Keya. "Wait for the review team's decision?"

"Their findings will only be a recommendation, but the chief constable will be under pressure to agree with them, and, as I said, he's expected to make his formal decision by the end of the year at the latest."

"In just a few weeks?" Suddenly, the reality of the situation hit Keya. "While I'm still on sick leave?"

"Yes," Inspector Evans agreed seriously, "which is why we might need to consider putting some options in place before the announcement."

"Like what?" Keya queried.

The inspector drew his lips together. Then he said slowly, "There are likely to be redundancies."

Keya remembered Zivah's suggestion to take the redundancy money and use it for the café. And she did enjoy running her café, but did she want to give up her police work forever?

"Or changes. And not just for those on sick leave," added the inspector.

Keya and Ryan stared at him.

Stan sat back and added, "Those close to retirement."

Keya yelped. "They'll sack you?"

"Possibly," replied the inspector. "And if not, it's clear that whatever reshuffle occurs after the review team submits their findings, there won't be room for a stuck-in-his-ways, close-to-retirement police inspector."

"But what will you do?" asked Ryan, sounding worried.

The inspector glanced at him and replied, "Like Sergeant Varma, I need to consider my options."

CHAPTER FIVE

After Inspector Evans had delivered the stark news about the review of Cirencester Police Station, and the possibility of Keya being pushed out of the force, she left her colleagues to finish sampling and evaluating the festive afternoon tea.

She decided she needed some fresh air, so she left the café by the side double doors, which led out onto the covered patio area, popular with customers in warmer weather.

The River Coln flowed ominously below. It was swollen, reaching high up the riverbank, and was dark in colour after the recent rain.

Usually, the water soothed her as she followed the path to a single-storey building, but not today. The purpose-built structure housed the Waterwheel Deli, which her youngest sister, Maitri, ran.

After a successful summer selling fresh vegetables, local products, and ice cream, trade had slackened off, and Keya wondered if people's interest had waned and they'd moved on to the next hot new thing.

Inside, all was quiet, and she rang the bell on the counter.

Maitri stepped out of the rear office and looked disappointed when she saw her oldest sister.

"Slow day?" asked Keya.

"Very. I'm not sure if it'll be worth opening in the New Year.

Perhaps we should wait until spring, when the café customers use the outdoor seating area."

"Why don't you think people are coming?"

"Because we're a bit remote, and they have to make a special trip. It's OK if they're visiting the auction house or antique centre in the summer and have time to look around, but in the winter, with the colder weather and the shorter days, people just want to get home. Other farm shops do OK, but they tend to be near towns or beside busier roads."

"What do you want to do?" Keya asked.

"Can I think about it?"

"Sure." Keya felt even more despondent as she left Maitri and returned to the café.

She wasn't the only one looking glum. Gilly Wimsey was sitting alone at a table, nursing a cup of tea. Usually so vibrant, bustling around with ringlets of her bright orange hair falling across her face and covering her equally brightly framed glasses, she looked forlorn.

Glancing up, Gilly saw Keya and said, "You look as if you need a cuppa too. And I could do with the company."

"I'll get you both a fresh pot," said Zivah as she walked past, and Keya sat down opposite Gilly.

"The antique centre not doing well?" enquired Keya.

"It's ticking along," replied Gilly. "But I haven't had time to concentrate on it. Do you remember when Dotty was here, and we did the Ten Days of Christmas promotion, and she served tea, coffee, and mince pies?"

"Yes, I do. And there was a real energy about the place."

"Exactly, and now it's flat. I haven't even had a chance to think about Christmas decorations."

"That was something I wanted to discuss with you," Keya said.

"Go ahead. Maybe it'll help me decide whether or not to decorate the centre."

"My team suggested a natural theme and decorations made out of paper, wood, and natural materials. Monica wants to decorate the tree with gingerbread men."

"Real ones?"

"That wasn't her suggestion, but perhaps we could," Keya considered.

"You don't need to do much in here to make a difference, but the antique centre is huge."

"Then why don't you concentrate on the front entrance? If people feel more festive when they walk in, you've achieved your purpose. And I noticed some of the stallholders have decorated their own areas. Why not encourage the others to do the same?"

"That would certainly save a lot of work. What do you suggest we put up?"

"Some fairy lights on the front wall. And what about a Christmas tree? We could buy two or three. One for the café and the others for the antique centre. They make a statement and are less fiddly to decorate than hanging streamers or other decorations."

"That's a good idea. I'll task Thomas with finding and buying the Christmas trees. And perhaps he can also see to the lights."

"How is he?" Keya asked.

"Much happier at sixth form college than he was at school. He says it's more grown-up, and as the children are treated as young adults, they have more respect for their teachers and each other. Or at least most of them do. There are still those who try to bully Thomas, but at least he has some friends and usually, he ignores the bullies."

Keya was pleased Gilly's son was finding his last year at school more palatable than the previous year.

"Gilly, Keya," said Aunt Beanie perfunctorily as she strode past them, heading directly to Norman's drinks counter.

Gilly's gaze followed her aunt, and then she turned back to Keya and asked, "You don't think something's happened to Uncle Cliff, do you?"

Aunt Beanie's husband had been in a nursing home for nearly two years, and he suffered from dementia.

"I don't think so. Norman mentioned something about a planning committee earlier," Keya responded.

"Oh!" Gilly's mouth opened wide as she made the sound.

"Is it important?" Keya asked.

"Yes, to Dotty at least. She's been waiting months to receive the decision and can't start renovating and converting the barn into her antiques shop without it."

Keya looked across at Aunt Beanie, who was gesticulating with her hands, and Norman, who placed a teapot on a tray which Zivah picked up and carried across to Keya and Gilly's table.

"What's the matter with Aunt Beanie?" Keya asked.

"Something about planning conditions. She keeps asking Norman what they mean."

"Let me speak to her," Gilly suggested. "Perhaps we can help."

Gilly pushed back her chair as Keya poured tea into two clean cups and Zivah left to find a third cup and saucer.

"If Norman's right, what am I going to tell Dotty?" implored Aunt Beanie as she followed Gilly back to Keya's table.

"Come and have a cup of tea and tell us all about it," suggested Gilly, who looked and sounded more like her usual motherly self.

Zivah placed a cup and saucer on the table before heading to the café entrance to greet an elderly couple who'd just entered.

As Keya poured another cup of tea, Gilly asked, "What decision did the planning committee make?"

Aunt Beanie placed stapled sheets of paper on the table and said, "They approved it, but subject to conditions."

Gilly picked up the papers and started reading them as Keya sipped her tea and Aunt Beanie regarded Gilly.

Turning the page, Gilly continued to read and then she stopped and appeared to reread a section.

Licking her lips, she looked up at Aunt Beanie and said, "It isn't good news for Dotty. You can convert the barn, but any use has to be ancillary to the farm."

"That's what Norman said, and that antiques won't count, unless they're vintage farm implements and the like which we can argue we're selling off."

"He's right. You could still use it as a retail unit, but it would need to be a farm shop, or I think you'd get away with a café. I'm not sure what other uses would be considered ancillary. Did the committee give you any indication?"

"They talked a lot about fruit, when we only have a few trees and bushes, and vegetables. There was a discussion about yoga and Pilates classes …" Aunt Beanie's voice trailed off.

"I don't see how they're connected to farming," said Keya.

"Quite. But they're all the rage at the moment, unlike antiques. Which should be, as selling them is a form of recycling."

Frowning, Aunt Beanie picked up her teacup and sipped from it. She sighed. "That's better. And what were you two discussing when I walked past?"

"Christmas decorations," Gilly replied.

"Can't say I'm feeling much festive cheer," commented Aunt Beanie.

"Neither am I." Keya told them about the police review and the possibility of permanently losing her job. Then she turned to Gilly and asked, "What were you worrying about when I sat down?"

"George."

"Oh!" This time Aunt Beanie was the one to open her mouth and voice the single word.

"Your sister? I haven't seen her for a long while," Keya said.

"Precisely. Dad and I have been running the auction house, which is why I haven't had enough time for the antique centre, but it's all coming to a head now."

"What is?" enquired Keya.

"Her marriage," replied Aunt Beanie. "Or more likely, the end of it."

CHAPTER SIX

On Wednesday afternoon, Keya was serving two ladies a pot of tea with slices of iced Christmas cake when she felt her phone vibrate in her pocket.

She checked that her customers had everything they needed before moving to stand beside the exposed brick wall of the café to take the call. It was Sujin.

"Busy day?" Sujin asked when she answered his call.

"Not bad. A steady stream of customers, which is how we like it. What about you?"

"I'm helping the Tewkesbury station. Thieves have been targeting garden sheds and taking all sorts of things from a motorbike, to unwrapped Christmas presents, and the wine one householder had bought for Christmas Day. I'm now forensically working through some of the evidence."

"I hope you can help. It must be unsettling for people to feel their properties aren't safe."

"Especially if they have children or pets around," added Sujin. "But on a cheerier note, are you still coming to our gig tonight?"

Sujin, as well as being a crime scene technician for Gloucestershire police, was a fiddle player in a band called the Celtic Twisters.

They played modern and traditional Celtic folk music, and their popularity in the area was growing, with an increasing number of requests to play in local pubs, village halls, and at events held in the Cotswolds and further afield.

"Remind me of the details?" Keya responded.

"It's at The White Hart in Stratton, so not too far away. I think Ryan and Millie are coming, so they'll keep you company."

Although Keya knew the other band members, when they were playing, she often found herself sitting alone. But she didn't mind, as she enjoyed listening to the music and was still mesmerised by the speed at which Sujin's bow travelled over his fiddle.

Sujin continued, "And Ryan mentioned that a house with a festive light display near him is attracting quite a following. I thought we might visit that first. Do you want to meet me at the station? We're only playing one set tonight, so we'll finish early and perhaps we can grab a bite to eat afterwards if you feel up to it?"

Thomas and Gilly arrived at half past four, carrying a Christmas tree wrapped in plastic mesh. While Gilly went in search of a stand for it, Keya let Thomas cut the mesh away, allowing the tree's branches to spring back into shape. She loved the fresh smell of spruce trees. It was a combination of citrus and peppermint and, overall, very Christmassy.

"Thanks, Thomas, we weren't expecting you to organise a tree so quickly. I don't think we've bought any decorations yet."

"Don't worry," Gilly said, manoeuvring her plump frame around tables and chairs while trying not to drop the cardboard box she was carrying, or the green stand balanced on top of it.

Gratefully, she placed her load on the table and handed the stand to Keya.

"I found several boxes of decorations in the cupboard with that. You can start with those and swap them for anything new that you buy. If you help Thomas with the stand, I'll check if any of the fairy lights work."

Alison assisted Thomas and Keya until the tree was settled in position beside the original mill machinery, next to the large window that looked out over the working waterwheel, and beyond to the River Coln.

They lit the waterwheel up when it was dark, so that would add to the festive feel.

"Be careful," warned Millie. Keya looked across the café as her young, blonde-haired front-of-house manager approached Gilly, who was fussing over a set of fairy lights.

"I don't understand why these don't work," Gilly said in a frustrated tone. "I only bought them last year."

Gilly picked up the bunch of lights, the black adapter, and the plug. She bent down towards an electric wall socket.

"Wait!" Millie called, "It might be the plug or the control box that's the problem. My uncle was electrocuted by a set of fairy lights a few years ago, and I read a warning on the internet that many lights bought online don't meet the electrical safety standards. Why don't you ask Norman to look at them in the morning?"

Norman had left early to accompany Aunt Beanie to a meeting with the planning officer to discuss the conditions imposed on planning consent for the barn.

Standing up, her round face flushed, Gilly admitted, "That's a good idea. The last thing I need is a fire, or someone being injured by dodgy fairy lights. But we could still put a star on the top of the tree." Gilly reached into the box and handed Millie a large gold star, which she gave to Keya.

Standing on a stool, Keya easily reached the top of the tree, but she struggled to attach the star. It slid onto the top branch but then drooped to one side.

"Try this elastic band," Monica suggested, standing beside the stool and reaching up towards Keya. "Or bend the branch in two and see if the star will slide onto it. We usually have a similar problem with our Christmas tree fairy."

As Keya attached the star onto the side of the top branch, securing it in place with a rubber band – she might ask Norman to redo it using some wire – Monica asked, "Can I order some of those gingerbread men decorations I saw?"

Monica, who was short and petite, and today was wearing a pair of green ballet pumps with bright red bows on the front, looked up at Keya excitedly.

"Won't someone try to eat them?" protested the dark-haired Alison.

"Hmm, that's a good point," Keya considered as she stepped down from the stool. "I do like the idea of gingerbread men, but ..."

"Real ones!" exclaimed Monica. "Mick and I could bake some. And perhaps the children who visit can decorate them?"

"That's a great idea," Keya agreed. "We should make a list of the ingredients and decorations we need."

An hour later, Keya glanced around the empty café. The tree did look a little forlorn, but she smiled as she imagined all the differently decorated gingerbread men that would soon adorn it.

After locking the café and the empty antique centre, she drove to Cirencester Police Station, parking in her old space.

Even though she'd only been working part-time for the past year as the rural engagement officer, and she'd spent a lot of it out in the community, she still felt at home as she entered the station.

Young Constable Warren Sparrow, who she'd worked with on her last case in the summer, was manning the front desk.

"Hi, Warren, can you let Sujin know I'm here?" The thin-faced constable placed a small headset over his mop of dark curls and tapped the computer keyboard.

What was wrong with picking up the phone? Or was this another change that had been made during her absence?

"Sergeant Keya's in reception," Warren said into the microphone attached by a narrow arm to his headphones. Looking up, he told Keya, "He'll be with you in five minutes."

Sujin arrived sooner than that and, ignoring the amused glance from Warren, he greeted Keya with a kiss on the lips.

Stepping back, he pushed his black-framed Wayfarer glasses up his nose and smiled. She thought how handsome he looked with his oval face, sandy-toned skin, and dark floppy hair, which gave him a schoolboy look.

He still spoke with the hint of a Scottish accent, which he'd acquired growing up in Glasgow.

"My car or yours?" asked Sujin.

"I don't mind, although I'm parked out front."

"Yours it is."

Keya drove out of the car park and back to the ring road, which was quicker than navigating the narrow one-way streets in the historic centre of Cirencester. But they weren't the only ones who'd come to view Gerald Sadler's Christmas light display.

As Keya drove steadily towards Zivah's modern brick house, she could already see the bright lights up ahead, beyond the queue of cars.

"I hadn't appreciated how popular this would be. Shall we give it a miss?" suggested Sujin.

"No way. I'm intrigued to see what's attracting so many people," Keya replied as she stared through her windscreen. "But we can park at Zivah's and walk the rest of the way. Is that all right?"

It was a chilly but clear night.

"Good idea," Sujin agreed.

Keya indicated and turned into Zivah's drive. The security light came on above the front door, which opened and an irritated-looking Aadi stepped out.

His face softened when he saw Keya's car and when she climbed out, he said, "I thought you were another one come to stare at the Sadlers' light display. Zivah didn't tell me you were popping by. Aren't you playing at The White Hart tonight?" he said to Sujin.

"I am," Sujin replied, as Zivah joined her husband in the doorway, cradling baby Kaami.

"We've come to see the lights," Keya admitted, "and find out what all the fuss is about."

"I'll walk down with you," said Zivah. "Let me grab my coat."

CHAPTER SEVEN

*Z*ivah appeared a few minutes later, wearing a long padded coat with baby Kaami strapped to her front in a baby carrier. He was dressed in a cute, quilted onesie with little ears on the fur-lined hood.

"Taking him for a walk is a great way to get him to sleep," Zivah said as they left the drive and joined other people walking along the pavement towards Gerald Sadler's light display.

"Is it always like this?" asked Sujin.

"It's been busier since Gerald's interview on Corinium Radio, and apparently, he added reindeer pulling a sleigh to his display yesterday."

The end of Limes Lane was choked with cars and, as they approached, they heard shouting. It sounded like Jackson, Gabrielle's partner, who lived in the first house.

"Move that car, will ya? It's blockin' me drive."

"Now I know why Ryan asked if he could leave his car in our drive," Zivah said. "This is chaos." She looked at her older sister.

"I'm on sick leave, remember?" Keya replied.

"But someone needs to do something," Zivah insisted as Jackson strode down his drive and glowered at the car blocking his entrance.

"Move!" shouted Jackson, as several of the onlookers turned to stare at him. "And the rest of ye can get lost, too!"

The engine of the car started, but there was nowhere for the driver to go.

When Jackson stormed out into the road and gesticulated at another driver, Keya realised she'd have to intervene.

"Excuse me, sir," she said, striding forward.

"What do ye want?" Jackson turned his anger on her.

"I'm a police officer, although not officially on duty at the moment." Which was true.

"Then what are ye goin' to do about this? I have me rights, ye know?"

"Yes, sir, I understand but …"

Jackson's face was puce as he shouted, "Don't ye dare tell me to calm down!"

"I was going to say that I need your help to move these cars, and perhaps you should call the council in the morning?"

"Why? I did that. After being left on hold for ten minutes, they told me there was nothing they could do."

Keya sighed. She suspected the council would wait until there was an incident, like the one that had been about to occur this evening, and then push the matter on to the police. "I'll see what I can do, but for now, we need to move these cars."

With Zivah and Gabrielle looking on, Sujin and Keya, with Jackson's help, backed up the cars blocking the street, allowing those at the end of Limes Lane to leave.

Just as they were finishing, Constable Sparrow arrived.

"I thought you were on front desk duty," Keya said as he approached her.

"The duty sergeant took over and sent me here after someone called in to say that a man was threatening drivers. Is that true?"

"One of the residents was blocked in, but we've sorted out the worst of the traffic blockage. Now we have to stop it happening again." Keya glanced at her black watch, realising she needed to drive Sujin to his gig.

Addressing Warren, she said, "Can you put police cones out on the right-hand side of the street to stop double parking, and do you have any red 'Access Only' signs?"

Keya drove Sujin to The White Hart pub.

"Will you be OK?" Sujin asked as he climbed out of her car.

"Yes, but I need to help Warren, and I still haven't had a chance to see the lights!"

Returning to Limes Lane, Keya once again parked in Zivah's drive. She pulled on the high-vis police jacket Warren had lent her and walked along the pavement back towards the festive light display.

As she did so, she knocked on car windows and asked the drivers stopped next to the yellow 'no waiting' police cones to find somewhere else to park.

"But we want to see the lights," insisted the driver of a car full of young men.

"You and everyone else," Keya replied. "But if you drive any further, you might get stuck here for the night. Find somewhere else to park and walk back to see them, like me."

Keya felt comfortable in her role, and the police jacket was like a shield and her badge of authority. When people saw her approaching, she sensed them taking control of themselves and cars started to drive away before she reached them.

She'd seen the 'Access Only' sign at the entrance to Limes Lane, and she passed another one, which Warren had placed fifty metres before the new houses.

On the opposite side of the road, she saw Aadi and Zivah speaking to Larry Shipton outside his bungalow.

Keya joined them as Aadi said, "This is getting out of hand. A few lights and visitors to see them is one thing, but this?" He indicated towards Gerald Sadler's house.

Keya blinked. Different coloured lights flickered and flashed, and the garden was packed with illuminated snowmen, elves, gingerbread houses, Christmas trees, and much more.

There was the huge Father Christmas Gerald had been attaching to the side of the house when she'd been out walking with Zivah on Sunday, and the new sleigh and reindeer on top of the roof. How had Gerald secured them up there?

The front door opened, and a beaming Gerald stepped out and waved to the crowd.

Larry sighed. "He thinks he's some kind of local celebrity. It's fair put Jackson's nose out of joint. Gabrielle is the only famous person he likes on the street."

"What do you think of the display?" Keya asked.

"I like it. It's fun, and it also annoys Bart, or Bartholomew, as he insists on being called, who lives on the end next to the church. He's a dreadful man, and so rude to his patient wife. She's a saint to stay with him."

"But don't the lights irritate you? How do you get to sleep?" asked Aadi.

"Gerald turns off the flashing ones and dims the others, so it's fine. The only run-in I've had over sleeping is with Jackson playing loud music and hosting parties which run on into the early hours."

"Neighbours," muttered Aadi as Zivah glanced at Larry.

She said, "You shouldn't be standing out here wearing just that jacket."

"Ah, stop fussing, lass. This old tweed coat has kept me warm for years. Besides, I don't want to miss the fun."

A lady picked up several sprigs of holly displayed in a basket on the wooden stand Larry and Ryan had built. Keya heard coins drop into the honesty box positioned next to the basket.

"Or the money," Larry grinned.

"Do you really trust people to pay you?" Aadi asked in surprise.

"I did, but the box has been emptier than I'd have expected the last couple of evenings, considering what I've sold." Larry scratched his chin. "That's one reason I'm out keeping watch tonight."

A young boy picked up a glass jar and Keya heard him exclaim, "Look mummy, it's got a picture of a bee on it."

"It must be local honey," said the woman, and more coins dropped into the honesty box.

Larry widened his stance in satisfaction.

Warren crossed the road to join the small group.

"You look like you need a cuppa, lad," said Larry. "Make sure nobody tampers with my honesty box while I put the kettle on."

Larry left them, walking down the broken concrete path to the front door of his bungalow. His garden was neat, and Keya admired the pink, purple, and red flowers growing in the borders.

"What's Gerald putting out now?" Aadi asked.

"It looks like a little inflatable elf," said Zivah.

Gerald weaved around the illuminated decorations he'd already installed and stopped beside a sign that read 'Santa's Workshop'.

Playing to the crowd, he held up the little green elf before placing it beside the sign and unwinding the flex. He held up the plug and then bent down.

BANG!

All the lights cut out.

The crowd stood silently, except for the odd gasp and cry of surprise.

"What was that?" called Larry, stepping out of his front door.

In the darkness, a woman screamed.

CHAPTER EIGHT

K eya blinked, her eyes taking time to adjust to the darkness. But it wasn't completely dark.

The streetlights, one positioned outside the church and another to her right, just beyond Jackson and Gabrielle's house, still glimmered, but they appeared dim after the blazing lights on Gerald Sadler's property.

"Help! Someone, please help me," a woman called again.

Unconsciously, Keya's feet started moving across Limes Lane, and as they did, her vision returned.

"Excuse me," she said, pushing her way through the crowd that had gathered beside the Sadlers' front gate.

"What's happened?" shouted a young male voice.

"The transformer was probably overloaded and cut out," Aadi called back.

Keya glanced behind her and saw Aadi and Warren following her path through the crowd. But was it more than just a power outage?

Glenda Sadler was standing over her husband, and she turned her ashen face towards Keya as she strode up the garden path. "I think he's been electrocuted. He won't answer me."

This was serious if Gerald was unresponsive.

Aadi stepped forward, holding a small torch, and asked, "Where is your fuse box?"

"Above the front door," Glenda replied in a confused tone.

"I'll isolate the circuit first, in case the power comes back on. Don't touch Gerald until I do."

As Aadi entered the Sadlers' house, Keya called 999, gave her police credentials, and asked for an ambulance to be sent immediately to Limes Lane.

"Is he OK?" called a woman from the crowd.

"He's not moving," shouted a man in response.

Aadi returned and nodded at Keya, who slowly approached Gerald.

"Is he breathing?" whispered Glenda.

Keya knelt down beside the prostrate figure and looked at his chest. No movement. She placed her ear and cheek over his mouth and nose. No sound of breathing or flutter of breath on her cheek.

Then she lifted Gerald's chin and felt for a pulse, but there was none.

"Aadi, can I borrow your torch?" she asked.

Taking it from him, together with the keys and the keyring it was attached to, she shone the light into Gerald's eyes.

No reaction.

He was dead.

Looking up at Warren, who had stepped closer, she said, "Can you go and ask the people who are watching what they saw? And take their names and addresses if you can. It will help with any investigation, and those who don't want to give their details will leave. It's an effective way of dispersing the crowd; they'll only ignore you if you tell them there's nothing to see and ask them to go."

Warren nodded, removed a tablet and electronic pencil from his pocket, and walked towards the crowd.

Is that another innovative change? Keya wondered, but she had more important things to concentrate on now.

She turned back to Gerald's body. Had he died from electrocution or from a heart attack? That would be for the coroner to decide during the post-mortem. For now, she needed to support and comfort Glenda while preserving as much of the scene as possible.

"Glenda. Are you all right? Can I help?" a female voice called.

Keya turned her head to see the woman from the house next door, beside the church, standing at the end of the garden path, holding a battery-operated lantern.

"Annie," called Glenda.

That was her name.

"Can I come in?" Annie asked Keya.

"I was going to suggest you take Glenda inside and make her a cup of tea, but there's no power," Keya said as she stood up.

"But what about Gerald?" asked Glenda anxiously.

Keya shook her head, and Glenda's shoulders slumped. Then the tears started. Gently, Keya led her to the garden path.

A camera flashed.

"Warren," called Keya sternly, "No photos."

Annie rushed up the path as Warren repeated, "No photos," and then Keya heard a shuffle, followed by a man shouting some expletives at him.

"Calm down," called another voice. "We don't want to be arrested."

"Here you are," Larry said, carrying a wicker basket up the path towards them. Inside it was a faded red tartan thermos flask, and cups tinkled against each other as he placed the basket on the ground. "Hot tea and shortbread biscuits."

Zivah called over from the gateway, "Can I help?"

Keya handed Aadi his torch as they moved to join Zivah.

Although the crowd had diminished, a few people were still standing around on the pavement, staring at either the dark figure lying in the garden or the group drinking tea on the path.

"You should take Kaami back. I think we use a different substation, so we should have electricity," Aadi said.

"And you should go with her," said Keya. "I really appreciate your help, but there's no point hanging about. It's going to be a late night."

"Will you have to stay, even though you're not technically working at the moment?" asked Zivah.

"As a sergeant, and the first on the scene, I should."

"Do you have your house key?" asked Aadi.

Keya patted her pockets. She had her car keys, but no house key. "It must be in my car," she replied.

"Take mine," said Aadi, passing the keyring with the mini torch on it back to Keya. "And that might come in handy."

"Thanks," said Keya, and Aadi put his arm around Zivah as they walked away into the gloom.

Keya was immediately joined by Warren.

"I got a couple of statements, but all they say is that Mr Sadler bent down to plug in his new elf illumination, and there was a bang and the lights went out. Which is what we saw."

"Yes," Keya agreed.

"And I called in the incident. Someone should be here to relieve us soon."

"I'm not sure we'll be able to leave, but the first thing we need to do is secure the scene."

"I'll get some crime scene tape," said Warren, and he moved away.

Keya stepped back into the garden and started assessing the scene.

Although she thought all the lights were off, that wasn't true. Several strings of fairy lights were still on, so they must be battery-operated. One set dangled from a small tree, another was wrapped around a bush, and two sets illuminated the front windows of the house.

The rest of the garden was dark and filled with eerie shadows cast by the unlit inflatable decorations.

The cause of death appeared obvious. Gerald Sadler's hand was still grasping the plug, and when she examined his body, she'd seen a partially buried cable, and two heavy-duty plugs with grey plastic covers.

"When is our power comin' back on?" shouted Jackson, and she looked across to see his red face staring at her from the other side of the garden fence.

A security light above his front door illuminated Gabrielle, standing on the top step wearing only a thin top and comfy jogging bottoms. She called across, "How will they know? They're not the electricity company."

Jackson's response was full of expletives about not being able to watch the football, but Gabrielle responded playfully with, "I know you can't watch the telly, but there are other things we can do in the dark, which will also keep us warm."

With a grin, she turned back into her house, and with a last glance into the Sadlers' garden, Jackson followed her.

Headlights glared and then dimmed as Keya saw the shape of an ambulance arrive. Too late.

The driver stopped when he saw her and lowered his window.

She said, "I'm sorry to waste your time, but our victim is past your help."

He wished her luck and reversed back the way he'd come.

Warren approached, carrying an assortment of items. "I have the tape, and some gloves and booties for you, and a protective suit for me in case you want me to start searching the crime scene. Sujin gave us a talk about how to do it without cross-contamination."

Something slipped from his grasp, and Keya picked up a packet of evidence bags.

"Very good, Warren. I'm impressed." And she was. He was being very thorough, even though she doubted there was a crime scene and thought that Gerald Sadler's death was either an accident or due to natural causes.

Warren beamed with pride.

Another car passed as they were erecting the inner cordon of the crime scene and turned into the entrance to Clutterbuck's Farm. She wondered if it was Ryan.

As they created an outer cordon between the pavement and the front hedge, Keya noticed that even though the group of onlookers had dwindled, several were still holding up their phones, no doubt recording their every move. Warren had been right to ensure procedures were followed.

When they'd finished erecting the cordons, Warren said, "Shall I start the scene of crime search?"

"Why not? But don't touch the body, the illuminated elf, or the power cables. I'm hoping Sujin will be here soon to examine those."

Keya was in a quandary. She didn't want to disturb Sujin while he was performing, and she didn't have the police authority to call him to the scene. She hoped someone who did had already contacted him.

"Ow!" cried a gruff Welsh voice. Inspector Evans had arrived.

CHAPTER NINE

"Who turned all the lights off?" Inspector Evans asked, rubbing his knee. Keya wasn't sure what he'd banged it against.

Joining Keya at the garden gate, he said, "Evening. You look at home. Is this a straightforward case?"

"I think so." Keya relayed the events of the past hour or so.

"And which one is the victim's wife?" asked the inspector, staring at Glenda, Annie, and Larry, who were still huddled together on the garden path, even though they'd finished drinking their tea.

Seeing the inspector's look, Larry gathered up the cups and flask. "If you need anything, you know where I am," he said, picking up his wicker basket and nodding at Keya and Inspector Evans as he passed them.

Approaching the two women, Keya said, "Glenda, this is Inspector Evans, who'll be in charge of your husband's case."

"But surely there's no need for that," said Annie. "It was an accident, wasn't it?"

The inspector looked confused.

"I'm Annie Beckett. I live next door, by the church," Annie said, stepping forward and holding out her hand. Keya noticed a rip in her down jacket, with the fluffy white filling poking out.

"Inspector Evans," the inspector replied, shaking her hand. He regarded her for a moment longer before turning to Glenda.

"I'm sorry for your loss, and I'm sure this is a straightforward case, but we still have to investigate for the coroner. I hope we won't have to leave your husband out here for too long, but we're waiting for our crime scene technician to arrive."

Inspector Evans glanced at Keya, but she wasn't sure what he expected her to do to speed up Sujin's arrival. Sujin would have to collect his kit from the police station, and someone would have to drive him there. Keya checked her phone to make sure he hadn't contacted her.

As she was looking down, Annie cried out, and the inspector caught her arm to steady her.

"Thank you, Inspector. I didn't see the edge of the path in the dark. Would you like me to stay with Glenda?"

Just then, the lights flickered back on.

"What the …" muttered Inspector Evans.

"That's better," Ryan said, walking up the path.

"I'm not so sure, Sergeant Jenkins," grumbled the inspector, shielding his eyes. "I presume you know Mrs Sadler and Mrs Beckett."

Ryan nodded.

"Please take them inside to get their statements. And turn these lights off," the inspector added.

As Ryan escorted the women indoors, Inspector Evans stood in the garden, shaking his head.

"Why?" he asked, baffled.

"Maybe it's some kind of creative expression," suggested Sujin, who had just arrived. "Sorry I'm late."

The inspector scoffed, though whether it was at Sujin's comment or his tardiness wasn't clear.

The flashing lights finally stopped, and Keya had to admit it was a relief. But standing amongst all the inflatables, some life-size, was surreal.

First, the reindeer on the roof and sleigh vanished into darkness, followed by the Santa climbing the side of the house. Soon, only the path and house lights remained on.

The front door opened, and Ryan called, "Is that better?"

"Perfect," Sujin replied.

"How did you get back to the station to collect your car?" Keya asked Sujin.

"Millie drove me so Ryan could return here."

"Sergeant, bring Sujin up to speed," Inspector Evans instructed before wandering back toward the road.

Keya asked Sujin, "Did you finish your set at The White Hart?"

"No, we were only two songs in when Ryan told me what happened. So, this is the creator of all this?" Sujin gestured at the now-shadowy garden and silent inflatables. "Did you see what happened?"

"Not exactly. I was standing outside Larry's house talking to Zivah and Aadi when I heard a bang, and the lights went out. I didn't realise anything had happened until I heard screaming. Glenda, I presume. I found her standing over Gerald's body. Luckily, she didn't touch him before Aadi switched off the power."

Sujin spotted Warren in a full barrier suit and smiled. "I see Warren is taking my talk on contamination procedures to heart."

"He is, but I told him not to touch the body."

"Then I'd better begin my examination."

Sujin suited up while Keya watched him carefully approach Gerald Sadler's body.

"I hope we're not here all night," muttered Inspector Evans, who had reappeared by Keya's side.

"This is interesting," Sujin called.

"What is?" Keya and the inspector asked.

"Someone's tampered with the control box. It looks like they converted it from battery to mains power."

"Cheaper to run, I suppose," mused the inspector. "But imagine the cost of running all these lights."

He slipped on protective covers over his shoes and pulled on latex gloves. "Let's take a closer look," he said, stepping inside the crime scene tape.

Keya watched as Sujin pointed out the control box, and the inspector bent down to examine the dual plug set, where a cable led to the 'Santa's Workshop' sign.

A bright light from the road indicated someone was still recording their movements. Was that an issue? The footage might be useful later, if the case became more complicated.

The inspector muttered something to Sujin before ducking under the tape and rejoining Keya.

"Anything unusual?" she asked.

"Apart from a garden full of inflatable Christmas characters?" he replied dryly.

"They're elves, sir."

The inspector rolled his eyes as the front door opened and Ryan stepped out.

"I've taken both women's statements, sir."

"Good, Sergeant. I think we've covered most things. I see Constable Sparrow is still examining the wider scene."

In his full barrier suit, Warren was crouched down, inspecting something on the ground.

"Where's my wife?" demanded a gruff voice, as Ryan rejoined Keya.

Keya looked down the path to see the bulky figure of Bartholomew Beckett, Annie's husband, approaching.

"Sir," the inspector said, stepping forward. "This is a potential crime scene. Please remain behind the tape."

"First these awful lights, now a dead body. How will this affect house prices?"

"I think we've more important concerns right now, sir. A man has just died," the inspector replied sternly.

Bartholomew ignored him. "I always said this display would be the death of him, and look, it was, wasn't it?"

"We can't jump to conclusions, sir. And you are?"

"Bartholomew Beckett. I live next to the church. I'm here for my wife, Annie."

The inspector relaxed slightly. "Ah, the kind lady comforting Mrs Sadler."

"Isn't that your job?" snapped Bartholomew. "I've been waiting for her to make my supper ever since the power came back."

The inspector tensed again.

Keya intervened, "Would you like me to tell her you're here?"

Bartholomew narrowed his eyes. "I …"

"It's all right," Annie called from the doorway. "I've put Glenda to bed with another cup of tea. I'll come home now and make supper, then bring something over for Glenda."

"That's very kind of you," said the inspector.

"Completely unnecessary," Bartholomew countered. "Your place is to look after me, not your neighbours."

"She's in such a state," Annie said, looking sympathetically at Keya, Ryan, and the inspector.

"You've been very kind, and I appreciate all you've done," the inspector said quietly.

"Annie, come on," demanded Bartholomew.

Annie smiled at Inspector Evans. "Thank you."

CHAPTER TEN

K eya arrived at Cirencester Police Station at half past eight on Friday morning.

Inspector Evans had asked her to come in to write up her report and, cryptically, had suggested she stay for Chief Inspector Greg's Friday morning coffee and chat.

She made herself a cup of tea and settled at her usual desk in the far-right corner of Inspector Evans' small, ground-floor team room. At least the recent changes hadn't involved moving her desk or, worse still, assigning it to another officer.

"Hi," Sujin said, standing in the doorway. "It's good to see you back. I hated seeing your empty desk."

"I'm just typing up my report. Were you late last night?"

While she had returned to Zivah's house, Sujin had headed back to the station with the evidence bags after the coroner's team had collected Gerald Sadler's body.

"No, I thought about starting my forensic examination, but I was too tired and didn't want to make mistakes. Besides, it's not like we have a killer to track down."

"No jumping to conclusions," came Inspector Evans' baritone voice from the hallway.

Sujin jumped slightly, then stepped into the room, allowing the inspector to enter behind him.

"Of course not, sir. I just meant this was a case I didn't have to lose sleep over."

"Quite right. But you will be working on it today?"

"Yes, sir. After I've run some tests I promised to do for Tewkesbury station."

"And when can we expect the post-mortem?"

"I'll need to check. I didn't flag it as a priority."

"Understood," said the inspector in a dismissive tone as he walked across to stand in front of Keya's desk. Looking down at her with an unreadable expression, he said, "If I were to ask the chief inspector if you could consult on this case in a non-frontline role, would that be acceptable to you?"

"Yes, sir. But is it really necessary? The case looks relatively straightforward."

"I'm thinking of you, Sergeant."

Keya wasn't sure what he meant, but although his gruff manner had put many people off, she'd always found the inspector to be fair and reliable.

"In that case, yes, sir."

"Very good." He moved towards his office door but turned and added, "And remember the chief inspector's coffee and chat at ten. You should be there for that too, Sujin."

The inspector entered his office, partitioned off from the rest of the room, and closed the door behind him.

"The chief inspector must be making an announcement," Sujin remarked.

"I thought so too. Maybe the inspector's insistence that I write up my report this morning is just an excuse to get me into the station. But while I'm here, I should get on with it."

"And I need to run those tests for Tewkesbury."

Just over an hour later, Keya, Ryan, and Warren were climbing a flight of concrete stairs, the central section covered with cheap blue nylon carpet, to the first floor. They entered a grey-walled room at the rear of the station.

Unfortunately, the decor was one thing that hadn't changed while she'd been on sick leave, Keya thought.

"Looks like a full house," whispered Stan Rowbottom as he joined their group. "I'm running a book. Two to one the station closes, four to one against..."

"Welcome, everyone," announced Chief Inspector Greg, standing with his back to the side wall. His bald head gleamed under the fluorescent lights. "It's great to see such a turnout, though I'm sure the confidential rumour of an announcement had something to do with it."

He smiled wryly before continuing. "Thank you for your patience and professionalism during the review. Many of you know I've spent a lot of time fighting for this station to stay open and serve Cirencester and the wider Cotswold community. I'm happy to confirm that, with your support, we will continue to operate for at least the next five years."

Everyone clapped, and beside her, Ryan whooped.

Smiling, the chief inspector raised his hands for calm. The noise subsided.

"That's not to say there won't be changes," he added. "I've seen some of the recommendations, but like you, I'll have to wait until the chief constable makes his announcement to know exactly what they are."

"Will there be redundancies?" called an older sergeant near Stan.

"Potentially, and there will certainly be reassignments to other stations."

Muttering filled the room. Chief Inspector Greg held up his hands again for silence.

"I know this isn't exactly what you wanted to hear, but change is inevitable. The important thing is that Cirencester Police Station remains open."

Though that seemed to be his main point, Keya wasn't sure it had reassured everyone. Many were still uncertain about their futures.

Without much enthusiasm for coffee or chat, Keya's team returned to their own room, accompanied by Stan.

Once they were settled with hot drinks and Mrs Rowbottom's white chocolate and cranberry cookies, Inspector Evans leaned against his office doorframe.

"We shouldn't underestimate how hard the chief inspector worked to keep this station open," he said.

"But?" suggested Stan.

The inspector gave him a wry smile. "There is one, and it's a big one for us. I've been given the nod that our team is likely to be disbanded, with major crimes being handled by headquarters in Gloucester."

He paused to let the news sink in, though it wasn't much of a surprise after their conversation at the café on Tuesday.

Keya realised he was right. It made sense that headquarters would want control over significant cases instead of leaving them to smaller, outlying teams.

"Will we be expected to move to Gloucester?" Keya asked.

Ryan glanced at her, colour rising to his cheeks.

"You knew about this, didn't you?" she said to him.

"I suspected," Ryan admitted. "Since I was promoted to sergeant, I've been considering my options. There isn't room for both of us on this team, as they say."

"So you've applied for jobs elsewhere?" Keya wasn't sure how she felt about it, but Ryan was a capable officer, and his skills would be valuable in many departments.

Ryan nodded. "I've applied for several positions, and I have an interview on Monday for one of my preferred options."

"What's it for?" Keya pressed.

Ryan flushed. "I'd rather not say in case I don't get it."

"Fair enough. I'm sure you'll be great," Keya said.

She glanced at the inspector, who averted his eyes.

"Ryan's not the only one considering his options, is he, sir?" she asked.

Standing up straight, Inspector Evans replied, "As soon as the review team arrived, it was clear there was no place for someone like me in the bright new world of Gloucestershire Constabulary."

"So, what are you going to do?" Keya asked, concerned that without his job, the inspector might lose his sense of purpose.

"Find a force that values my experience," he replied.

Keya was relieved that he still intended to work, though he hadn't said where. Perhaps Avon and Somerset Police? Or somewhere further afield? He had no family ties in the Cotswolds now that his mother was gone.

"And what about you, Sergeant?" he asked, turning his gaze on her.

"I … I'm not sure."

"I hope you've picked up on my hints that if you want to avoid being top of the redundancy list, you need to be planning your return to work."

"I see." Keya hadn't realised the hints were about that, but now it was clear she was a prime candidate for redundancy. "So, what should I do?"

"First, decide if you want to continue working for the police or if you'd prefer to take the redundancy package and focus on your café."

"I'm not sure." Ever since Zivah had suggested she take the redundancy money, something inside Keya had resisted the idea. "And if I don't want that?"

"Then you need to explore other roles," the inspector said. "I don't think you'll enjoy being one of several detective sergeants working on a range of cases at headquarters."

"No," Keya agreed. The commute alone would be a hassle, not to mention the fact she couldn't easily pop back to the café. "What about here at Cirencester?"

"I suspect it will mostly be custody work," said Stan. "Or handling car thefts, vandalism, or drunken students."

None of those options appealed to Keya, though she'd done her share of all three.

"What about specialising in another area?" Ryan suggested. "I've heard they're outsourcing more roles. You could work in a consultancy capacity or on call?"

"That's an option. But what could I specialise in?"

"Let's see what courses are available." Ryan tapped away on his computer. "Resource Manager. You'd deal with HR, governance, data planning, resource management…"

"Stop," Keya said. "That's not me. Too much paperwork and procedure."

Ryan scrolled further. "Here's another: Designing Out Crime."

"Don't you mean dining out?" joked Stan. "That's for the top brass."

Ryan read on. "It's about advising organisations like the London Underground, Network Rail, and construction companies on how to design or refurbish buildings to reduce crime."

"That sounds technical," Keya mused.

"I wouldn't mind doing that," said Stan. "Is it only open to serving officers?"

"It doesn't say," Ryan replied.

"Anything else?" Keya asked, feeling disheartened by the options.

Ryan scrolled again. "This might be more up your street: a course to become a Crime Scene Manager."

"I could see myself doing that," Keya said.

"It's quite technical, but I'm sure Sujin can help with the forensic side. You'd be eligible to work with various police forces and outside organisations like the British Transport Police and Military Police."

"I like the sound of that," Keya said. "And I could still run my café alongside it."

Ryan nodded. "I'll email you the details."

CHAPTER ELEVEN

That evening, Keya met Sujin at the Barn Theatre on the edge of Cirencester.

Once a private house with extensive stables and servants' quarters, the stone-built property had been requisitioned by a weapons components company during World War II, and a temporary, half-cylindrical-shaped Nissen hut had been built in its garden.

The Nissen hut still survived and, after many varied uses, had been converted into a professional theatre. Keya's friend, Dotty, had taken her there to see a play, and she was excited to be trying the award-winning subterranean restaurant in the old servants' quarters this evening.

Having returned to Zivah's to change into something more elegant than the jumper and trousers she'd worn to the station and café, she found Sujin already waiting for her at a table for two.

"Sorry, am I late? What time is the show?" Keya asked, as Sujin stood up to greet her.

After a quick peck on the mouth, Sujin said, "Don't worry, we have forty-five minutes, and I took the liberty of ordering for you from the pre-show set menu."

Keya was relieved that she had one less decision to make and was intrigued to find out what Sujin had ordered.

"And you look lovely," added Sujin.

Keya's cheeks flushed as she adjusted her blue embroidered tunic top and sat down.

"I didn't get a chance to see you before you left the station. How did your team take the chief inspector's news?" Sujin asked.

Keya told him about the discussion that followed the announcement.

"I suspected they already knew something. Ryan has been asking me about different positions and potential jobs. I wonder which one he's been selected to interview for?" Sujin pondered as a waitress brought them a bottle of water and two glasses.

"Would you like anything else to drink?" she enquired.

"No, water will be fine for the moment. Thank you," Keya replied. She figured there might be time for a cup of tea later, before the stand-up comedy show started.

"Have you heard anything about your position?" Keya asked.

Sujin glanced around before leaning forward and lowering his voice. "This is confidential."

Keya felt a flutter of excitement.

"They wanted me to move to police headquarters, but I'm not sure I want to. However, something else has come up that would mean a promotion. Quite a major one, actually. And I'd earn more money. There's only an outside chance that I'll get it and, as I said, it's all hush-hush for now."

"That's great," said Keya enthusiastically as the waitress returned, placing two cheese soufflés oozing with a chive and cheese sauce on the table.

"I hope this tastes as good as it smells," said Keya, picking up her fork and diving into her starter.

She leaned back in her chair. "Delicious."

Sujin smiled appreciatively.

They ate in comfortable silence for several minutes, savoring their food before Keya asked, "I suppose I should ask about Gerald Sadler's case. Have you been able to close it?"

Sujin shook his head as he swallowed. "Not yet. It's the control box that bothers me."

"Why?"

"Because I doubt it was the first time he'd converted one of his decorations from battery to mains power. But if it was, why try it out in front of all those people? What if it hadn't worked, and he'd made a fool of himself?"

"You mean instead of dying?"

"That's not what I meant. But the wiring is wrong, and that's what's nagging at me."

Keya paused before taking her next bite and asked, "You don't think someone else is involved, do you? That they deliberately tampered with the controls?"

"Look, it could have been a genuine mistake, but what I'd like to do is examine Gerald's other lights, their controls, and power sources, to see if this was a one-off."

Finishing her delicious starter, Keya pushed her plate to one side.

Sujin looked at her and said, "I don't want to jump to conclusions, and Inspector Evans made it very clear that I shouldn't, but I'd like to clear up this issue. That means returning to the scene."

"Now?" Keya asked as the waitress cleared their plates away.

"No, I booked these tickets three months ago. But what about tomorrow morning? We could go first thing before you head to the café. That is, if you're staying over tonight?"

"I am. Zivah and Aadi have been great, but I'd like to give them some time together. If that's OK with you?"

"Of course it is, and why not stay the whole weekend? Do you have to work all of it?"

"I suppose I am the boss." Keya smiled playfully as the waitress returned, setting down a wide bowl filled with gnocchi, herbs, and crispy kale in a creamy herb sauce in front of her. Sujin had chosen moules marinière, which arrived in a tall metal pot.

When the waitress left, Keya asked, "Do you have any other plans for the weekend?"

"I'd love a leisurely Sunday, reading the papers and enjoying a traditional Sunday lunch. And," he hesitated, "all this talk of change at the station has got me thinking about my life."

"That sounds serious," said Keya, stabbing a piece of gnocchi with her fork.

"It isn't meant to, but then again, I suppose it is. I do need to think about my future in case the position I'd like doesn't come through, or Gloucestershire Police makes me redundant..."

Keya gasped.

"Roles like mine are being outsourced to private companies. Chief Inspector Greg fought hard to get me appointed to Cirencester, but how long will I have a job in the police force?"

Sujin swallowed and then met Keya's gaze with a quiet intensity. "And... I guess I'm wondering if you see yourself in my future, too."

CHAPTER TWELVE

It was still dark when Keya woke up on Saturday morning, so she turned over and snuggled up to the still-sleeping Sujin.

Or at least she thought he was asleep until he muttered groggily, "I enjoyed last night. Thank you for coming with me, even though I know you didn't really enjoy the comedian."

She hadn't. It had been more like a comic routine aimed at drunken men in the pub than a mixed audience in a small market town in the Cotswolds.

The teenager who'd come on in a supporting role for the last part of the show had been much better, and he was the only reason she hadn't walked out.

"But it was fun to go and spend time together. And the food was lovely," Keya replied.

Sujin hugged her close and whispered, "Would you like a cup of tea? We'd better get up if we're to visit the Sadlers' house before you start work at the café."

Keya enjoyed the rejuvenating spray of the shower and then the hot cup of tea while she dressed. After a hasty breakfast, she and Sujin climbed into his Skoda Yeti, which was filled with equipment he might need to examine the crime scene.

"The only thing I can't take is a stepladder, so I hope I can borrow one from Mrs Sadler if I need to," Sujin said as he turned the ignition key, and the engine started.

Twenty minutes later, they entered Limes Lane, driving past Zivah's house where a downstairs light shone behind a closed curtain, even though it was now light outside.

Sujin slowed as they reached the end of the lane.

"Where's all this rubbish come from?" Sujin asked as he noticed the drink cans, crisp and sweet wrappers, and the empty branded containers from nearby fast-food and takeaway outlets.

They parked at the side of the road before they reached the new houses, and Keya climbed out, staring at the rubbish. "It looks as if someone had a party."

The door of Larry Shipton's house opened, and Keya thought he was about to shout at them, but instead, he raised his hand in acknowledgment. He ducked back into his bungalow as Keya and Sujin walked toward the Sadlers' house.

Keya crossed the road to speak to Larry, who reappeared carrying a grey dustbin bag.

"Now don't tell me I should separate the recycling from this rubbish," he protested. "I wouldn't do it at all except Glenda's in no state, and Jackson and Bart complain loudly, but do they lift a finger to help?"

"Where's it all come from?" Keya asked.

"Gerald's lights are more famous, or should I say infamous, since he died. Ryan had to come and tell people to go home last night after I finally persuaded Glenda to turn the lights off at midnight. There was a bit of a scuffle as some of the youths had been drinking."

As if to make his point, Larry bent down and picked up an empty yellow beer can.

"I'm not sure what to say about that," Keya responded, "except that the best way to stop visitors is to take the lights down, or at least switch them off for a few evenings."

"Aye, I suggested that to Glenda, but she felt she should keep the display on in Gerald's memory. If there's a similar crowd tonight, she might find Bart or Jackson taking them down for her."

"I'm surprised you're not bothered by it all. After all, you've been living here quietly for years," Keya said.

"I'm doing jolly well with my stall," Larry admitted. "My takings have been good the last few nights. I'm still not sure what happened at the beginning of the week."

He frowned before adding, "And I believe in leaving people be. As long as that developer stops pestering me, I'll be fine. I ain't selling, and that's final."

Larry looked defiant, and Keya didn't get a chance to ask him anything else as Sujin called, "Can you help me?"

"I better go," Keya said to Larry.

"What are you doing back here?" he asked.

"Sujin wants to check the controls on the lights to see if Gerald had altered any of them."

"He liked to tinker around," mused Larry. "Even came to ask me for this and that after he stopped complaining about my place being an eyesore."

Keya walked up the garden path and knocked on Glenda's front door as Sujin, wearing shoe coverings and gloves rather than a full forensic suit, picked up a candy cane inflatable garden decoration.

Knocking again, Keya still didn't receive a response, and she wondered if Glenda was at home or just still in bed. She felt rather guilty disturbing her if she was sleeping, especially if she'd been bothered late into the night by rowdy onlookers.

But Sujin did have a case to investigate, and hadn't the inspector asked her to consult on it?

The door opened a fraction, and a nervous female voice said a hesitant, "Hello."

"Morning, Glenda. It's Sergeant Keya Varma from Cirencester Police. Zivah's sister. I'm here with my colleague who wants to check some of the garden lights. I thought I should tell you what he's doing and check that you're OK."

"Come in," Glenda invited politely, if not enthusiastically, and the front door opened wider.

Keya stepped inside as the plump, dressing-gowned figure of Glenda was already walking away. She entered a room on the left.

Keya stopped and looked around. Even though Glenda and her husband had only moved in during the summer, the property had a cluttered feeling about it.

She glanced through a door to her right and guessed it would be described in a brochure as a study, but it looked more like a workroom.

An open toolbox stood on the table near the window, and a screwdriver had been left next to pieces of wiring and a roll of duct tape. Empty cardboard boxes and plastic packaging were spilling out of a wastepaper basket.

Glenda appeared in the doorway through which she'd disappeared and said, "That's Gerald's room. Or it was," she sniffed. "Tea or coffee?"

"Tea for me, please."

"And for your colleague?"

"I'm sure he'd appreciate a coffee." Keya followed Glenda into an open-plan kitchen diner. She had a feeling this was Glenda's space.

It was much tidier than the hallway and, although one countertop was filled with appliances, each of them seemed to have their place. Canvas print photographs adorned the walls.

Keya stepped closer to study one grouping of wonderful sunsets and noticed a younger Glenda standing with a mixed group of people.

Behind her, Glenda said wistfully, "Thailand. I visited on an organised trip. I loved travelling and spent most of my wages on it after my fiancé was killed. Gerald and I didn't marry until we were both in our forties."

"And did he join you on your trips?" Keya asked as she turned to face Glenda.

Handing Keya a cup, Glenda replied, "Gerald never travelled further than Edinburgh."

Keya wondered what the couple had in common.

"But he enjoyed country walks and city breaks until he became obsessed with something that took up all his time and ..." Glenda's words trailed off, and Keya wondered if she was going to add 'money.'

Glenda continued, "It was metal detecting for a while, then building and flying drones, and of course, more recently, his Christmas light display."

Keya had the feeling that Gerald's hobbies hadn't left much time for Glenda. "And what about you?" she asked.

"I went back to work full-time, three years after our marriage." Glenda smiled fondly.

"What were you doing?" Keya asked, trying to keep her tone conversational.

"I was a laboratory technician. Nothing very grand, but I liked my work and my colleagues. We had a pub quiz team and a group of us would play bingo regularly."

"That sounds fun," Keya said.

"It was, but I had to give it up when we moved here."

"And why did you move?"

"Gerald's great retirement plan. Move to the Cotswolds, start walking again and visit local pubs, but ..." Again, Glenda's voice trailed off.

"But that didn't happen?"

"I know we've only been here a few months, but apart from my neighbours and your sister, I hardly know anyone. Gerald spent his entire time 'making his mark in the community', as he put it, by organising his display."

"Perhaps it would have been different after Christmas, with the warmer spring weather," Keya suggested.

"Perhaps," but Glenda didn't sound convinced.

"And what will you do now?"

"Now? I've no idea. I thought I should continue the display for Gerald, but it was so noisy and busy last night. And both Jackson and Bart threatened to report me to the council. So I'm not sure what I should do." Glenda looked pleadingly at Keya.

"I'll see if I can organise a uniformed officer to be on duty tonight since, technically, this is still a crime scene."

"Crime scene?" Glenda's voice rose in pitch.

"What I mean," said Keya in a soothing voice, "is that until we establish exactly how Gerald died, this is an ongoing investigation. It's why Sujin, my colleague, is here assessing the scene further."

"So this is just routine?" Glenda asked, still sounding concerned.

"It is," Keya replied. "And nothing for you to worry about."

At least, Keya hoped that was the case.

CHAPTER THIRTEEN

Keya left Glenda to get ready for the day and carried Sujin's cup of coffee outside. She found him examining the plug and control box for a set of standing lights shaped like snowflakes.

Watching him from the garden path, Keya asked, "Have you found anything?"

Looking up, Sujin replied, "Several sets of lights had been altered to run off mains electricity, and it looks as if Gerald converted them himself."

"That makes sense. There are tools on a table in the study inside."

"Why then," said Sujin, placing the snowflake control box and plug on the ground, "did he make a mistake with the elf controls?" He joined Keya, removing his gloves and taking hold of the mug of coffee.

"What do you think?" asked Keya cautiously. She really didn't want to get involved in a complex investigation in the run-up to Christmas.

"That before I can advise the inspector or the coroner that this was a death by misadventure, we need to consider if another person was involved."

Keya groaned. "You mean a murder investigation?"

"No, well, yes. I suppose so. But it's most likely that Gerald's death was an accident or one of his own making."

"But?"

"But we wouldn't be doing our jobs if we didn't investigate it fully. It doesn't sit right with me that someone with Gerald's experience would wire the control box incorrectly by mistake."

"He could have, though," reasoned Keya. "He didn't come across as a very tidy or organised person, from what I saw of the house."

"Still," Sujin pressed.

"OK, I get it. We're to treat this as a suspicious death until proven otherwise."

"Hello," a voice called. "Can I come in?"

It was Annie from next door, smiling broadly as she held up a round pie dish.

"You're OK as long as you stick to the path," Keya replied.

Annie's thin frame walked up the path as she said, "I've made Glenda a quiche, which she can pick at. I'm sure she doesn't feel like cooking at the moment. And she must be exhausted after last night. Bart won't stop complaining about all the people and the noise they made."

She lowered her voice. "But he never does anything about it. Poor Larry is the one left to clear up. I must go and help him."

"When did you move in?" Keya asked, switching into her police investigation mode.

"We reserved the house off-plan. Bart liked the idea of living next to the church, but it took us a bit of time to sell our old house. You know what these property chains are like."

Keya didn't, but she nodded anyway.

"So it was mid-September when we finally moved in. Glenda and Gerald were already here, and Gabrielle and Jackson moved in at the beginning of October." Annie lowered her voice again as she confided, "I think Gabrielle had been filming somewhere exotic."

Keya smiled, although she wasn't sure what Annie considered exotic, but her tone and phrases were endearing, and Keya couldn't help warming to her.

"I get the sense that Glenda's been a bit lost since she moved in. She hasn't found it easy to make friends, and she doesn't garden or do anything like that. I did take her to have a look around Rodmarton

Manor and its gardens, but Bart didn't like that. He thinks I should be integrating with the county set. Me!" Annie giggled.

"What are you standing around talking to the police for?" called an irritated male voice.

For a fleeting moment, Keya thought a shadow crossed Annie's face, but then she smiled again and apologised, "Bart doesn't think it looks good having the police here. Now, I must give this to Glenda," and she carried the quiche up to the front door.

Keya heard another door open, and she looked round to see Gabrielle picking her way across her lawn, wearing her pink fluffy heeled slippers and a hoodie top over a pair of white jogging pants.

By her side, her Treeing Walker Coonhound, Chief, bounded alongside her, nose to the ground, sniffing eagerly at every corner of the garden.

"Hi," Gabrielle called across the fence, resting a hand on Chief's head as his tail wagged excitedly. "Poor Gerald. Do you know what happened to him?"

Sujin looked at Gabrielle, then quickly looked away, his discomfort evident as he muttered, "I should get back to work."

Smiling sympathetically at Sujin's discomfort—since Gabrielle was very attractive and did little to hide her assets—Keya took his half-drunk cup of coffee and manoeuvred her way around to the fence dividing the Sadlers' property from Gabrielle and Jackson's.

"Hi," Keya said. "We haven't been formally introduced."

"You're Zivah's sister," Gabrielle said. "She's so lovely, and little Kaami is gorgeous. I'm trying to persuade her to let me introduce him to my agent. He'd be a perfect baby model."

"Oh, yes, that sounds interesting," Keya responded, losing her train of thought and thinking how sweet Kaami would look in an advert for baby food or nappies. But would he be embarrassed by them when he was older?

Directing her thoughts back to the investigation, Keya replied, "I am Zivah's sister. Older sister, and I'm also a police officer. Sergeant Keya Varma."

"Isn't that great? Even in a sleepy town like this, there are ethnically diverse police officers. Do you find it difficult?"

"Find what difficult?"

"To be accepted. Especially as you're a young, attractive woman. Have you ever thought of modelling?"

Keya wondered why this interview kept wandering off track.

"No, I haven't thought of modelling, and no, I don't find it hard working locally. But it wasn't easy when I first became a police constable. And what about you?" she said, once again attempting to return to her line of questioning. "Is that a trace of an accent I hear?"

"Spanish," Gabrielle replied. "I'm from Seville. It's such a wonderful city. Have you been there? You should…"

"And when did you move here?" Keya asked before the conversation derailed again.

"England, five years ago, but I was fed up with London. I thought moving to the countryside would be fun, and I saw all these adverts for the Cotswolds."

Keya wondered how long the Cotswolds, and Cirencester in particular, would hold Gabrielle's attention.

"When did you move here?"

"At the beginning of October," Gabrielle replied, concurring with Annie's earlier statement.

"And how well did you know Gerald?"

"Not well. I speak to Glenda more. She's rather lonely, I think. But Gerald was always busy with this or that. He should have given his wife more time and attention."

"Why?" Keya asked, wondering if Glenda had been having an affair. Now that would put a different spin on the investigation.

"Then she would have been happier and given him what he needed, and he wouldn't have spent all his time doing that." She indicated toward the Sadlers' garden.

Keya felt deflated. A potential line of enquiry had been snuffed out.

"So you don't think the marriage was a happy one?"

"Who knows? They are old," said Gabrielle dismissively.

When did people start to look old to someone like Gabrielle, who was in her late twenties? At fifty? Or forty? Glenda must only be in her early sixties, although Keya knew from the police report that Gerald had been sixty-eight.

"But they were always polite to each other. No shouting like Jackson and me. No passion." Gabrielle pursed her lips. "I think I'll invite her to our Christmas Eve party. Maybe she'll meet a real man."

"Gabrielle," Jackson called.

"Must go!" and Gabrielle tottered away, with Chief wagging his tail, following behind her.

Sujin removed his gloves and overshoes as Keya returned to the path.

"Finished?" Keya asked.

"Yes, but I'll take those with me." Sujin pointed to several large evidence bags.

"I should head to the café. What are you going to do?" Keya asked, suspecting she already knew the answer.

As she thought, Sujin replied, "Check what I've gathered against the controls for the killer elf."

CHAPTER FOURTEEN

Keya spent the rest of Saturday at the Waterwheel Café.

"Look at all these gingerbread men," Monica said, standing with Keya beside the Christmas tree.

Following Norman's suggestion, Keya had bought a new set of fairy lights instead of risking the ones Gilly had purchased the previous year, and they twinkled against the darkness gathering beyond the large glass window.

Norman had also secured the gold star to the top of the tree, which was, as Monica had pointed out, covered with a range of decorated gingerbread men, stars, houses, and baubles. Mick had found some cookie cutters and created the variety of shapes.

"They're perfect," continued Monica as she watched two girls, around ten years old, sitting at the decorating table. The girls laughed as they used the coloured icing pens, silver balls, and coloured glitter to create their gingerbread shapes.

Gilly joined Keya and Monica and said, "At this rate, you'll either need a second Christmas tree or we can use the gingerbread creations to decorate the trees I put up in the antique centre today."

Gilly's cheeks were rosy, and her orange ringlets danced in front of her face as she spoke.

"Lovely idea," Monica replied in a distracted voice. "Excuse me." She crossed the café to meet Ryan, who had just arrived.

Turning back to Gilly, Keya asked, "Is business improving?"

"Yes. After speaking to you, I suggested to the stallholders that they decorate their spaces, and many of them have. But what I'm most relieved about is the Christmas auction, which I had been dreading organising."

Keya waited for Gilly to continue.

"I spoke to Dotty, and she gave me an idea to raise awareness and encourage people to submit festive-themed lots to sell by offering a reduced sales commission."

Gilly lowered her gaze and admitted, "I didn't tell Dad that bit."

But then she looked up again and enthused, "But I'm sure he won't mind. We've already received new submissions following my email yesterday, and a local farmer has asked if we can sell his Christmas trees in the parking area on auction day, which will raise more money. And The Crown in Cirencester asked if we'd auction a Christmas lunch for eight people, which I think is a fabulous idea."

Keya agreed that it sounded positive. "Is Dotty going to help?" she asked.

It depends on when she returns from Leicestershire. The Yuletide market brought out more than just festive cheer.

"Oh no! What happened?" Keya asked, hoping Dotty wasn't caught up in yet another murder investigation.

"Didn't you see the news about the young entrepreneur being hit by an ice sculpture?"

"That was at Dotty's market?" Keya's fears had been realised. She felt sympathy for her best friend and hoped she'd be able to get back to the Cotswolds in time for Christmas.

"Ah, here's Aunt Beanie with Uncle Cliff and his friend Edith from the nursing home. She promised to join them for your special festive afternoon tea."

"How is Uncle Cliff?" Keya asked.

"Not so good. Edith is doing a great job of keeping him going, but he rarely seems conscious of what's happening around him and, in his frustration, he's starting to get violent. But he still enjoys his food, and it's during meals that he's most lucid. Aunt Beanie is hoping he'll enjoy this special treat."

Millie escorted Aunt Beanie's group to a table close to the Christmas tree, where Gilly joined them.

Gilly's Uncle Cliff had run Meadowbank Farm as his family had done for generations. But he and Aunt Beanie didn't have any children to take it on, and when it became too much for Aunt Beanie to manage on her own, Norman had persuaded her to lease it out to contractors.

Converting the barn for Dotty to run her antique shop would have provided additional income, and perhaps it still could. Keya wondered how Norman and Aunt Beanie's meeting had gone with the planning officer.

Christmas tunes played in the background as the two young girls carried their gingerbread decorations across to Keya. One of them asked, "Where do I put my house?"

"That's lovely," Keya enthused regarding the gingerbread decoration. "Why don't you hang it on this side, where it will stand out, as there aren't many others?"

Both girls hung their Christmas decorations, and then Keya stepped to one side so their proud dad could take a photo of them beside the tree.

As they returned to their table, Keya heard Millie request, "If you post that on social media, can you add the hashtag Waterwheel Café?"

Well done, thought Keya. She was always forgetting those sorts of marketing details.

The café had a lovely feel about it, and it wasn't just the Christmas tree and hessian bunting Millie had hung that morning with Merry Christmas on it. It was the smell of hot chocolate mixed with orange and cinnamon, the chatter of animated voices, and the happy smiles of her customers.

She felt upbeat as she crossed the café and approached Norman's drinks counter, where Ryan was leaning as he read a newspaper resting on the countertop.

"It says here," said Ryan when the noise of the milk frother Norman was using subsided, "that every year, around a thousand people are injured by their Christmas tree while fixing decorations to the highest branches."

"You hear that, Keya?" said Norman when he turned and saw her approaching. "Make sure you stand on the step when you rearrange the children's gingerbread decorations."

"And don't water the tree with the lights on," cautioned Ryan. "In the past ten years, twenty-six people have died doing that."

"What did they expect?" muttered Norman, as he placed two cappuccinos on a round, black tray.

"And three hundred and fifty people are hurt each year by fairy lights," continued Ryan.

"Now, I'm surprised that number isn't higher." Norman squirted whipping cream onto a mug of hot chocolate, pushed a chocolate flake into the thick mound, and sprinkled mini marshmallows over the top.

It looked very appetising, especially when Norman finished it off with a drizzle of chocolate sauce.

Bryonie, Alison's daughter, who was working today, carefully lifted the tray and carried the luxurious drink away.

"That's why I told you to buy new lights from a reputable source," Norman said, bringing Keya's attention back to the subject of Christmas mishaps.

He filled a teapot with hot water. It was decorated with images of holly leaves and berries. Keya had spotted it in the antique centre and bought it on impulse for the café.

"And there's that poor man who died plugging in his Christmas lights in Cirencester," added Norman.

"Gerald Sadler, one of my neighbours," Ryan responded dully.

"Is that so?" Norman shook his head. "What a tragic accident."

Keya felt the heat rise in her face.

Norman stared at her. "It was an accident?"

Ryan's eyes widened.

"Probably, but Sujin isn't happy about the way the controls were wired. We were back at the Sadlers' house this morning, and Sujin's been at the station all day checking other lights he gathered from the garden."

"And?" Ryan pressed.

"I don't know. I haven't heard from him. But I did speak to Glenda, Annie, and Gabrielle while I was there, and to your neighbour, Larry."

"Larry Shipton?" Norman queried. "That's a name from the past."

"Do you know him?" Keya asked.

"I worked with him when he ran a garden and grounds maintenance company. We'd call him and his lads out if we needed a tree felling or a branch lopping off. They'd also cut some hedges when I was too busy."

Norman had previously worked at a local country house, Windrush Hall, for the Duke of Ditchford before he'd died.

"And do you know if he was ever involved in any unscrupulous behaviour?" Keya asked.

Norman didn't answer straight away as he concentrated on preparing two more luxury hot chocolates, which he added to the tray with the holly teapot.

"Do you think I could have one of those?" Ryan asked, eyeing the hot chocolates.

Norman checked the screen on his tablet and replied, "After I've prepared a couple more coffees."

He unclipped the circular coffee filter, added ground coffee, and pressed it down with a wooden-handled tamper. Clipping it back onto the machine, he placed two cups beneath the dual spouts before answering Keya's original question.

"I liked Larry. He was old school but shrewd. The man I knew wouldn't deliberately set out to harm someone, but there was talk…"

As thick dark liquid ran into the two cups, Norman switched on the milk frother, and their conversation paused.

When the hissing and steaming finished, and Norman was pouring the hot milk into the two cups, he continued, "Larry thought one of the lads was stealing from him, as pieces of equipment kept going missing, or the lad would say they were broken, but wouldn't return them to be repaired. Then a man ended up in hospital electrocuted by a lawnmower he claimed to have bought from the lad who worked for Larry."

"Do you think Larry had anything to do with that?" Keya asked.

Norman picked up a red cup and started to prepare Ryan's hot chocolate, adding hot milk rather than water to a superior brand of drinking chocolate.

"Nothing was proved, but it wouldn't surprise me if he had. As I said, Larry was a wily old fox."

Keya considered Norman's information as Ryan took the full cup Norman handed him. He removed the chocolate flake, licking cream from it.

"What about electrics?" Keya asked. "Would Larry know his way around a plug and set of light controls?"

Norman placed his arms on the counter and leaned forward, considering Keya. "What are you getting at?"

"Nothing," Keya replied innocently.

Ryan hid his reaction by spooning marshmallows and chocolate sauce into his mouth.

Frowning, Norman said, "This is my final word on Larry, as I don't want to implicate him in anything. But yes, he did know his way around electrics. He once helped me put up an electric fence after his Lordship offered to rescue some rare sheep, and Larry was a dab hand with the battery and wires."

Keya glanced across at Ryan, who shrugged and said, "I guess we need to interview Larry again."

CHAPTER FIFTEEN

K eya and Ryan agreed that Larry Shipton wasn't likely to abscond and that they could wait until Monday to speak to the inspector about interviewing him.

That meant Keya could enjoy a leisurely Sunday, as planned, at Sujin's rented house in the small town of Highworth, on the edge of the Cotswolds.

Both Alison and her daughter Bryonie were working at the café, and Millie was joining them later in the morning after she and Ryan had completed whatever crazy run or cycle route they'd planned for their "relaxing" Sunday morning.

Sitting on the sofa, with her feet resting on the pine coffee table, Keya was enjoying browsing the food and drink section of the Sunday newspaper, which Sujin had already popped out to buy. Next to her, with his feet also on the table, Sujin was reading the main section of the paper.

"It says here that there's an increase in mortality rates at Christmas and New Year," Sujin remarked.

"That's hardly surprising," Keya replied. "Although I'd have thought January and February would have more deaths as the weather is cold, which must cause problems for older people."

Sujin continued, "Heart attacks are actually the biggest cause of death due to what the article describes as 'festive fear.'"

"What's that?" Keya asked, picking up her mug of tea.

"Something women are more likely to be susceptible to, as they become overwhelmed, rushing about tidying the house, buying and wrapping presents, and organising food. And forty-nine per cent of them say they have suffered accidents while cooking the Christmas meal, including being burnt by hot fat or cut by a knife while preparing vegetables."

Sujin looked at Keya and said thoughtfully, "Maybe that's why my mum buys everything ready-prepared in foil packets and puts it in the oven or in the microwave. And there's virtually no washing up."

"Sounds sensible," agreed Keya, who couldn't imagine her mother doing anything other than creating elaborate festive meals, although Christmas wasn't a special time for her.

"Wow," said Sujin, reading more of the article. "Over six hundred million units of alcohol, equivalent to two hundred and sixty-five million pints of beer, are consumed by Brits each December."

Keya's eyes widened. "I've dealt with my fair share of drunken and disorderly behaviour, but that seems extreme. To compensate for those who don't drink or drink only a little, everyone else must consume a huge amount."

"Think of all the Christmas parties, and the excuse of 'it's OK, I'll have a dry January,'" Sujin reasoned.

Keya shook her head.

"OK, I'll stop soon, but listen to this," said Sujin. "I'm not sure of the timescale, but a survey has been carried out that reports over 400,000 turkeys have been burnt at Christmas, and half a million people have had a fire in their homes. And over 700,000 people have been injured in a sales rush while shopping."

"At least that number will be lower now, unless you count injuries to people's hands when trying to grab the best online deals. But can we change the subject?"

"Sure," Sujin replied, sounding despondent.

"I did find it interesting, but Ryan was also talking about accidents and injuries at Christmas yesterday, and it's rather depressing."

"I know. We should change the subject."

"What would you like to discuss?" Keya asked in an upbeat tone.

Sujin lowered the newspaper and considered her. "Me. Us," he replied.

"Go on." Keya hadn't expected the conversation to take such a serious turn so early on a Sunday morning.

"You know I told you that a position had come up, which would mean a promotion if I got it?"

"Yes. Have you?"

"I was offered the job yesterday, but…"

"That's great news! Why the 'but'?"

"It's not in Gloucestershire, or even in England. I've been invited to work back in Glasgow."

"Oh." Keya tried to hide her disappointment.

"But I'm not rushing into anything yet," Sujin insisted, picking up her hand.

It sat limply in his as Keya said, "But you are considering it? As you said, it's a promotion, and I know how excited you are about it."

"I am, but I wanted to speak to you before I make my decision."

"I don't want to hold you back, and if this is your dream job…" Keya's voice trailed off.

"But you wouldn't move to Glasgow with me?"

"Scotland?" Keya gasped.

Sujin laughed. "They may speak funny, but it isn't a foreign country. Yet. They may hold another referendum," he mused.

"But that would mean leaving here. My job, if I have one, the café, and my family. And what about my friends?"

"They could visit, but it's what I thought. Your roots are too deep here to up and leave with me."

Keya nursed her half-finished cup of tea, pressing her lips together. She did like Sujin and truly enjoyed spending time with him. He liked trying new things, though never anything too far out of her comfort zone.

He was also a great musician. He'd have to leave the Celtic Twisters, but surely he'd played with other bands before leaving Glasgow. That city was his home, just as Gloucestershire and the Cotswolds were hers.

She felt Sujin's hand squeeze hers, and in a soothing voice, he said, "You don't need to say anything else. And I'm sorry to spring it on you like this, but I needed to gauge your reaction, and I have it now. This is where you belong, and just as you don't want to hold me back, I don't want to take you away from the life you've built here."

She looked up at him, her chest brimming with gratitude for his understanding, but with a nagging tug on her heart that she might lose him.

Sujin sat and smiled. "But, you know, there's more to life than work. And what about a walk through Cirencester Park, followed by a cosy Sunday lunch beside the fire at The Bear?"

CHAPTER SIXTEEN

As the café was closed on Monday morning, Keya arrived at Cirencester Police Station just before nine to write up her unofficial interviews from Saturday morning. She found Stan in the small ground floor kitchen.

He asked, "Fancy a brew?"

"Yes, please. It's chilly out today."

"I'm considering putting a bet on for a white Christmas," Stan declared.

"What are the odds on that?" Keya asked.

"They've moved into six to one from eight to one in Cirencester, but lower in the north and in Scotland."

Scotland. That reminded her of her discussion with Sujin the previous day. Although she had enjoyed their bracing walk and tasty lunch, it hadn't been the relaxing, carefree day she'd been anticipating, and she'd returned to Zivah's on Sunday evening rather than stay the night at Sujin's.

"Everything OK?" asked Stan.

"Oh, yes. It's just this review, and our future at the station."

"I suspect I'll be OK, but you and the rest of the team?" Stan shook his head.

"Do you know what the inspector is considering?"

"I do." Stan smiled superiorly but then admitted, "But I promised not to tell anyone. Not that they'd believe me."

Keya narrowed her eyes, intrigued. "Does it involve leaving the Cotswolds?"

"Not just the Cotswolds." Stan wrinkled his nose before handing her a mug of tea.

As she carried it along the blue nylon-carpeted corridor, she wondered if she was close-minded and dull not to consider moving to Glasgow with Sujin.

"Good. Sujin said you'd be coming in this morning," Inspector Evans greeted her. "He's asked me to call a team meeting."

Keya followed him into their room. Ryan, wearing his police uniform, was already tapping away on his computer at the desk opposite Keya's, next to the inspector's office. Warren, also in uniform, was seated at the desk next to Keya's.

As she sat down, Stan entered, carrying a tray of mugs, which he placed on the empty desk next to Ryan. He started handing them out as Sujin walked in and looked around.

"We're all here," said Inspector Evans, standing in the open doorway to his small office. "I presume this is about the Gerald Sadler case. When is the post-mortem due to be carried out?"

"Later this morning, as long as there aren't any pressing new cases," Sujin replied.

"After which, the coroner will want our initial findings. Which are?" The inspector looked at Sujin.

"That this is either an accidental death, death by misadventure, or murder."

Inspector Evans raised his eyebrows but didn't respond verbally.

Sujin continued, "The cause of death is almost certainly a heart attack, as a result of being electrocuted, although we'll have to wait for the post-mortem to confirm that. Witnesses, including Sergeants Varma and Jenkins, heard a loud bang and then all the lights in the vicinity went out."

"A short circuit," suggested the inspector.

"Caused because the control box of the illuminated elf was incorrectly wired."

"The manufacturer's fault?" queried the inspector.

"No, the original controls were battery operated. They were altered to use mains power, at least that was the intention, but the wiring was wrong."

"So who wired the control box?" the inspector asked, although Keya wasn't sure if it was a rhetorical or actual question.

Sujin responded, "That's what we need to work out, sir."

The inspector looked around the room.

It was Warren who asked, "Couldn't he have made a mistake and electrocuted himself?"

"I've examined other lights from the Sadlers' garden, which had the same modification, and they were wired correctly. I can't guarantee this one wasn't a mistake. And, of course, Mr Sadler could have done it on purpose," Sujin suggested.

"Suicide," considered the inspector.

"Surely not, sir," reasoned Keya. "He'd recently retired and only moved into his new house this summer. And, according to his wife, he'd been planning the Christmas light display for some time. I think it was the highlight of his year."

"So suicide is possible, but unlikely," the inspector stated. "And if he didn't deliberately wire the control box incorrectly, that also rules out death by misadventure. So if Sujin is pouring cold water on an accident..."

"Murder," groaned Ryan. "On my street."

"Succinctly put, Sergeant. And as you know the likely suspects, where do you suggest we start?"

Ryan looked at Keya, who replied, "Larry Shipton."

Ryan drove a squad car back to Limes Lane, as Keya wasn't covered by police insurance to drive while technically still on sick leave.

"I really hope Gerald's death does turn out to be an accident," Ryan complained. "I don't like the thought of arresting one of my neighbours for murder."

"Does that bother you?" Keya asked. "Arresting guilty people."

Ryan considered her question before replying, "I don't mind when it's criminals. People who I know have deliberately done terrible things. But so often the people we send to jail just made a stupid decision in the heat of the moment, or they were pushed too far by someone else's behaviour. Most of them aren't bad people."

"But where do you draw the line? Do you let someone go because they've been a lifelong member of the Women's Institute or donated regularly to a local animal charity?"

"No. But you know what I mean," reasoned Ryan.

And Keya did. But she was also clear where the legal, if not moral, lines were, and there were consequences for those who crossed them.

But she wasn't sure Ryan agreed as he sat rigid, staring out of the windscreen.

"Is this one of the reasons you decided to look for another position?" Keya asked, curious about Ryan's job applications.

"I didn't want to work for the murder team at headquarters," Ryan responded.

"I visited them and, even without our extra workload, they're juggling so many cases. How could I give individual cases the focus they need? And there wasn't really a team atmosphere. It felt more results-driven and impersonal, with no discussions like we tend to have."

Keya understood Ryan's misgivings, and suddenly she felt grateful for being part of Inspector Evans' team.

She'd applied for the position as few people had wanted to work with the gruff inspector, and she'd thought that her age, gender, or race might unofficially preclude her from other departments, even though nobody would officially admit they were a factor.

Although the inspector's team was small, they'd successfully solved many cases, sometimes with the help of her friend, Dotty, a competent amateur sleuth. And Ryan was right.

They'd needed time and space to look at some investigations from different angles. And often, they'd had to be sensitive towards the people involved, even those they discovered were guilty.

She realised that there was no way she wanted to move to headquarters, even if she was offered a place.

"You're quiet," said Ryan.

"I was thinking over what you said and how I'd feel about moving. I agree, I don't want to go to Gloucester. And talking of moving, don't you have an interview today?"

Ryan's cheeks coloured. "This afternoon. So I'll need to finish before lunch if I'm to make it on time."

"Can't be too far then," mused Keya, still wondering what and where the position was.

The colour in Ryan's face deepened, but he didn't say anything as he indicated right and turned into Limes Lane.

CHAPTER SEVENTEEN

Allll was quiet on Limes Lane as Ryan brought the patrol car to a stop outside Larry Shipton's bungalow.

Keya stepped out and pulled her scarf tighter against the biting wind that swept across the fields behind Larry's home.

"Morning," she heard Larry call. Glancing around, she spotted him standing in the doorway of a greenhouse attached to the side of the bungalow, its glass panels stained green and brown.

Instead of opening the garden gate, Keya walked up the drive on the left side of the property, heading toward a stand-alone garage. She wondered if it held a rusty vintage car or perhaps was crammed with things Larry couldn't bear to throw away.

Ryan accompanied her, and they followed a gravel path from the drive to the front of the greenhouse.

"You two still working Gerald's case?" Larry asked in an unconcerned tone.

"Yes, we need to take your formal statement, as there are some irregularities in respect of his death."

"Irregularities?" repeated Larry. "Like what?"

"We're not at liberty to say," Keya replied, hoping she didn't sound too official.

"Like that, is it?" Larry replied in an aggrieved tone. "Then, as this is a formal interview, should I have a solicitor with me?"

"You're within your rights to have a solicitor present, but then we'll need to conduct the interview down at the station." This wasn't going as planned, and Keya was concerned that she was alienating Larry.

Ryan stepped forward and said, "We just need a formal statement, Larry. For the record. And to clear up a few points. I'm sure you understand. It's not like one of your neighbours electrocutes himself every day."

"So that's what killed him."

Before Keya could answer, Ryan said, "We think so, but we're still waiting for the results of the post-mortem."

Larry appeared mollified and asked, "What do you want me to tell you?"

Keya realised they'd have to be careful with how they questioned Larry, as he was likely to pick up on any hint of suspicion they had about him being involved with Gerald's death, so she started with, "Do you know anyone who would wish to harm Gerald?"

Larry leaned back and whistled. "This is serious. Do you think someone did for him?"

She must be out of practice, Keya thought. This interview was still not moving in the direction she wanted it to.

"At this stage, Larry," Ryan reassured him, "we have to cover all bases. For the coroner, you know."

Larry still eyed them suspiciously as he said, "Gerald and Glenda have only been here a few months. They moved from Bristol after Gerald retired. I've no idea if he upset anyone there."

"Have they had many visitors since they moved?" Keya asked in a more conversational tone.

"Now you would have thought they would, wouldn't you? Bristol's not that far away, but I haven't seen anyone. And poor Glenda, she's been rather lost. Annie and I have tried to encourage her to take an interest in her garden, but it's not really her thing. Mind you, she's been a godsend helping me out with my computer and buying and setting up a new printer for me. Why does everything have to be online these days? Just booking a doctor's appointment is complicated."

"And Gerald? Did he help with any odd jobs?" Keya asked.

Larry scoffed. "Him? Nah. He was too wrapped up in himself and his Christmas display. If Glenda needs a picture hanging or some shelves putting up, she asks me." Larry smiled proudly.

Keya knew she needed to tread carefully with her next line of questioning. "So you and Glenda have become friends?"

"Aye, we have." Larry looked at Keya and then exclaimed, "Hey! Not in the way you mean. My Janet has only been in the ground a year."

"I wasn't suggesting anything, but if you and Glenda are close, she might have let slip something about Gerald and their previous life, or any worries or concerns she had."

"I think the biggest concern she had was moving here with Gerald and leaving her job, trying to make new friends."

"Was it Gerald's idea to move?"

"I believe so, and I know he took money out of his retirement fund to buy that house. His dream was to live in the country, which is why I don't understand why he wanted to cover his house in all those lights and huge inflatable decorations. But each to their own."

"Did you ever see Gerald and Glenda fight?"

"No, not those two. Now, if you take their neighbours, Jackson and Gabrielle. They're always screaming at each other or throwing something. She broke a perfectly good vase the other day. Bits of it shattered all over the pavement."

Keya realised she was unlikely to get any more insights into Gerald and Glenda from Larry today. She took a deep breath. Time to tackle Larry's past and delve into the story Norman had told her.

"Larry, I do need to ask you a few questions about your past."

As expected, Larry became defensive, leaning back and crossing his arms, but she ploughed on.

"I understand you ran a garden maintenance business."

"So what if I did?"

"Nothing, it sounds like a very useful and practical enterprise, but not something you'd do on your own. You had people working for you?"

"Sometimes," Larry responded evasively.

Keya felt as if she was moving through thick treacle as she tried to coax answers from Larry. She'd had enough of being subtle.

"Look, Larry, I heard that you once had an employee who you suspected of stealing from you, and then one of your lawnmowers went missing, and a week later a man ended up in hospital, electrocuted by the stolen lawnmower."

"Now who told you about that?" Larry asked, sounding amused. He removed his cap and scratched at his white hair.

"That doesn't matter, but I can't help drawing similarities between the two cases."

"What? A man electrocuted by a lawnmower over twenty-five years ago and Gerald being electrocuted by his Christmas lights?"

"Yes. Exactly that."

"I didn't have anything to do with the lights, and as for the lawnmower, well, nothing was ever proved," Larry said as he shifted his weight from one foot to the other.

Keya narrowed her eyes as she regarded him. "That doesn't mean you didn't do it."

"Look," Larry said, pulling at his ear.

"So what if I taught someone a lesson for stealing from me. The police refused to do anything about it when I reported the thefts, so I took matters into my own hands. I didn't mean for anyone to get hurt. And the gentleman only spent a couple of days in hospital. Then he was right as rain. And that good-for-nothing lad I'd employed didn't bother me again, even after I got rid of him."

Keya decided to continue with her direct approach to questioning Larry. "Did you alter or touch the controls on Gerald's illuminated elf?"

Larry stared at her. Speechless.

Then he muttered, "What are you talking about?"

"I shouldn't really be telling you this, but it looks as if the controls on the lights had been tampered with, and you know your way around machinery and electrics."

"Aye, but no more than the next man," Larry protested.

As the next man, or the next-door neighbours, were Jackson and Bartholomew, Larry probably did know more than them.

Larry continued in an aggrieved tone, "Anyway, how could I? That was yet another new figure that Gerald had bought, and I didn't know about it until he held it up for the crowd of onlookers to see. If I'd wanted to do anything, it would have been easy enough to fiddle with one of the lights or decorations already in his garden."

Which, Keya thought, was a reasonable point.

"But if I did have an issue with Gerald, I'd have dealt with it the old-fashioned way and talked to him."

CHAPTER EIGHTEEN

"Cooee," called a voice, and Keya turned to see Annie Beckett walking up Larry Shipton's driveway, carrying a blue pot with what Keya recognised as pansies in it.

Keya turned back to Larry, who was still standing in the open door of his rickety greenhouse, and said, "Thank you, and I'm sorry if my questions were a little uncomfortable, but we're just trying to get to the truth."

"Aye, no bother. I know you and Ryan are only doing your jobs."

"What job is that?" asked Annie, brightly.

"Making enquiries into Gerald's death, Annie," Larry stated.

"Oh." Annie blinked, swallowed, and looked momentarily taken aback before she smiled. Was it a forced smile? And said cheerily, "Any news about that?"

"Not at the moment," Keya replied. "But I'm afraid we do need to ask you some questions."

Annie shivered.

"Why don't I take that?" said Larry, eyeing the flowerpot. "Mildew, I presume?"

"Yes, I just can't seem to get rid of it." Annie handed the flowerpot to Larry, who turned and entered his greenhouse.

"Why don't you two come home with me?" Annie suggested. "No

point answering questions in the cold when we can sit down with a nice cup of tea and a slice of Christmas cake."

Keya would certainly welcome a cup of tea, and Ryan brightened at the mention of cake. They left Larry's and crossed the road, entering Annie's neat property. Plants were already established in the borders, and two tall pots either side of the front door contained brightly coloured flowers.

"Do you mind taking your shoes off?" Annie asked as they entered an immaculate hallway. "There are crocs and slippers you can put on in that basket."

Inside the front door, there was a second mat, and to one side of it, a five-level wooden shoe rack and a colourful basket containing slip-on shoes.

Keya removed her shoes and slipped on a pair of flip-flops. Ryan took off his boots but declined the offer of shoes. Keya doubted he'd find any in his size, but as they followed Annie across the polished hardwood floor, she hoped he wouldn't slip in his socks.

The house was exactly the same layout as Glenda's next door. Keya hadn't been able to look into the study, as the door had been closed, but the hallway was neat, with a narrow table displaying a colourful red plant and a pair of silver-framed photographs.

"Nice poinsettia," Ryan said.

That was the name of the plant, Keya remembered.

They entered the kitchen and dining area, and Ryan excused himself and moved toward the front window as Keya looked around.

The arrangement and furnishing of the room were very different from Glenda's traditional format.

It was modern and simplistic, with no appliances on display. The only worktop was the white marble-topped island, which was illuminated by four pencil-shaped pendant lights.

Annie pressed a switch, and a panel opened upwards, revealing a gleaming chrome kettle and an expensive-looking black Italian coffee machine.

"Tea or coffee?" asked Annie.

"I'm a tea drinker, thanks," Keya replied, wondering how she'd manage with such a minimalistic designer kitchen. She'd probably break something.

"Sorry," Ryan apologised, rejoining them. Turning to Keya, he said, "I've called Warren to take over from me and drive you back to the station."

Because Ryan had his interview, Keya remembered.

"You're not leaving just yet, are you?" Annie sounded disappointed.

"No, and I'd love a coffee and, if I may, a slice of cake. I'm not sure if I'll have time for lunch."

"Then I must make you a sandwich. You can't work on an empty stomach."

"Actually, I have a job interview," Ryan replied, looking sheepish.

"Then you definitely need to eat."

The fridge was hidden behind another panel, and while Annie prepared the drinks and a chicken and coleslaw sandwich for Ryan, Keya continued to look around.

Beside the entrance door, there was a neatly arranged message board. Keys hung from hooks beneath it, and letters and flyers were stacked up behind a horizontal chrome bar.

Pinned to the board with chrome pins was the programme of December church services, a schedule of events for The Barn Theatre, a calendar with neatly written notations, and a handwritten list of names.

She recognised some of the names, including her friend, the former rock singer, Jay Newton.

To herself, she muttered, "I must contact Jay," but the overweight man she knew as Annie's husband, Bartholomew Beckett, heard her as he entered the kitchen.

"You know Jay Newton?" he asked, sounding surprised.

"Yes, I've helped him in the past with some charity work and suchlike," Keya replied evasively, as her relationship with the present owner of Windrush Hall was none of this man's business.

"Then you must introduce us." The man stepped closer to the board and, catching his stinking breath, which smelt like rotten eggs, Keya moved away quickly.

"We could invite him and the Oakhams a week on Saturday, Annie."

Keya glanced at Annie, whose face showed an expression of irritation, which was quickly replaced with a bland smile as her husband turned toward her.

"See to it, will you? And where's my eleven o'clock cup of coffee?" demanded Bartholomew.

"Just coming," she replied sweetly.

"I don't need anything to eat," he snapped, eyeing the sandwich Annie was cutting into four neat triangles.

"This is for Sergeant Ryan."

Bartholomew wrinkled his nose, and Keya heard him mutter something about having to feed the police as well as put up with them as he stalked out of the room.

"Sorry about my husband, he's trying to close a complex business deal before Christmas." Annie placed Ryan's sandwich on a white plate and pushed it to the far side of the island.

As she returned her attention to the message board, Keya wondered how often Annie had to apologise for her husband. Looking down the list of names, which she realised were the great and the good of the Cotswolds, she asked, "Do you know all these people?"

"Goodness, no," Annie replied, "But Bart believes we should make an effort to meet people, and as we are the new ones to the area, we should make the first approach and invite them for dinner."

Keya looked at the calendar where the names of three ladies she recognised were jotted down. They included the chief constable's wife. "I can see you're making a start. It can't be easy meeting new people."

"Oh, that's just one of my ladies' lunches. Bart says they don't count."

Keya raised her eyebrows as she turned away from the message board.

Ryan was seated on a white leather-topped stool, tucking into his sandwich.

"Here's your tea," Annie said as she placed a china cup and saucer on the island. "Will you excuse me for a minute while I take Bart his coffee?"

Keya knew she could be clumsy and didn't want to risk marking one of the white stools, so she stood next to Ryan and sipped her tea.

"It's smart in here, isn't it? Like a picture in one of those magazines my mum sometimes reads."

"But it's so clinical and impersonal," Keya remarked. "Where are the family photographs, or children's paintings?"

"I don't think they have kids," said Ryan before taking another bite of his sandwich.

"That's not the point. But you're right. It's just like a kitchen you'd see if you opened Country Life or an interior design magazine."

She hadn't heard Annie return until their host said, "Bart would be so happy to hear you say that. And he has invited Cotswold Life to write a piece about it. The marble was brought all the way from Italy."

Annie tried to sound proud, but her words were hollow. It was probably the spiel she gave to all her visitors.

Keya cleared her throat. Time to get down to business.

"We need to ask you a few routine questions about Gerald Sadler," Keya said, trying a different approach from that which she'd taken with Larry, and not mentioning that they had any concerns about his death.

"Yes, OK," Annie replied. She pulled out a stool and moved it round to the side of the island, where she sat down, a cup of coffee in front of her.

"He and Glenda moved here before you?"

"Yes, in August."

"So they've had longer to get to know people."

"Not really." Annie leaned forward, placing her elbows on the island top as she disclosed, "They never have any visitors. Not even family, or people they knew from Bristol, where they used to live. And Glenda is struggling to make friends. She's come to some of my ladies' lunches, but I always have the feeling she's bored by the small talk. I don't think fashion, or the antics of famous people, interest her. I tried to persuade her to come to one of Gabrielle and Jackson's parties when Bart was away, but she looked at me as if I'd suggested flying to the moon. And it was such fun."

She whispered in a conspiratorial tone, "I did meet Jay Newton there and his lovely friend, Tracy, but don't tell Bart." In a normal voice, she disclosed, "And I also met a young artist, Finn, and his friend, a local art dealer, Jarrod Wilcox."

Both of whom Keya also knew from previous cases.

"And a gay couple who present dog programmes on one of the TV channels. They were such a hoot."

"Did Glenda or Gerald go to any other of their neighbours' parties?"

"Oh, no, and Jackson refused to invite them after Gerald complained to the local council about the noise from one of them."

"So, is it fair to say that Glenda and Gerald didn't have many friends?"

"None," stated Annie, "apart from us neighbours."

CHAPTER NINETEEN

When Ryan received a message from Warren that he'd entered Limes Lane, Keya thanked Annie and accompanied Ryan outside.

"I like Annie," Ryan said, mirroring Keya's thoughts.

As Keya watched Warren attempt to park his police car, she wondered about Annie and Bartholomew's relationship.

Annie was so outgoing, sociable, and fun. Whereas Bartholomew came across as abrupt, rude, and – oh – his breath! How could Annie put up with it? Perhaps he was worth a fortune, and she was with him because of his money. But Keya had the impression that Bartholomew, rather than Annie, insisted on the designer items and that he was, frankly, a social climber.

Annie was probably more at home in her garden, but her gregarious nature and willingness to try new things meant she had met people in the area.

Keya couldn't get her head round their relationship.

"Right. I'm off," Ryan said as Warren approached them.

"Good luck," Keya said, and Ryan smiled nervously at her.

"Remember, few police officers have your experience, as you've worked on some diverse cases over the past few years. And we couldn't have done it without your technical skills and your professional attitude."

As she spoke, Ryan stood taller and squared his shoulders.

"So go in there confident, but not arrogant. And be yourself."

Ryan smiled gratefully at her. "Thanks. That means a lot."

"But you still won't tell me what the job is?" Keya pressed.

"No. Not yet." Looking serious, Ryan left and walked towards his car.

"Morning, Sarge," Warren greeted her.

Keya wasn't sure about the casual use of her rank, but she let it go.

"The first interview won't be easy," Keya stated. "We need to go back to the Becketts' and speak to Bartholomew. He's a self-important man, so I doubt we'll glean much information from him, but if he tries to fob us off and say he's too busy, we must stand our ground. And after him, we need to interview Gabrielle and Jackson."

At the mention of Gabrielle's name, Warren's face brightened.

Returning to the Becketts' house, Keya exchanged her shoes for flip-flops, and Warren pulled a pair of forensic overshoes from his pocket and pulled them over his boots. Perhaps he was brighter than she'd given him credit for.

"Ryan's suggestion," said Warren before Keya knocked on the study door. Annie knew she was returning, but Keya had the impression she didn't want to be involved with anything that meant disturbing her husband.

"What?" called an irritated-sounding Bartholomew from behind the closed door.

Keya opened the door and walked in. She'd decided against apologising for doing her job and instead said, "Mr Beckett. We need to ask you a few routine questions about Gerald Sadler and his death."

Her approach with Bartholomew was to be direct, not to mention that there were any suspicious circumstances, and to stand her ground.

"Not now. I'm working," he objected.

"So are we, and this case involves a death. I'd have thought you'd want to help your neighbour."

"Which one? Glenda? I'm not even sure what she does. And as for

Gerald. Even after his death, those dreadful lights are still creating a spectacle. I moved here from London for some peace and quiet and to live the country life. Not to have carloads of gawping yokels congregating each night, shouting, jeering, and leaving rubbish behind. That's what you should be putting a stop to, not worrying about Gerald's death. That's over. He was electrocuted. Now sort out those lights or I will."

Bartholomew was red in the face when he finished his rant.

Levelly, Keya responded. "A death, especially one which has not been explained, takes priority over neighbourly disputes, and …"

Bartholomew cut her off. "Neighbourly disputes! Do you know how much this house cost and how much the value has decreased because the street is lit up like Blackpool illuminations?"

Keya knew he was referring to the famous lights of an English seaside resort.

"And what other explanation do you need for Gerald's death? He was electrocuted. And by one of his own hideous decorations." The colour in Bartholomew's face changed to a deeper shade of red as he raised his voice.

Keya took a deep breath, composing herself before replying, "As I said, we're just doing our job. Your office overlooks the Sadlers' property," she said, glancing at a small side window. "Did you see anyone in Gerald's garden or notice any visitors?"

"You're right, I can see into Gerald's garden. Just look at that oversized Father Christmas climbing up the side of his house! Any bigger, and it would be hanging over our fence. I've half a mind to get rid of it myself."

"If you could answer my question, sir?" Keya pressed.

"Did I see anyone? No, I did not. But I was working in London on Wednesday and Thursday morning, and I didn't return home until mid-afternoon. But let's face it, Gerald and Glenda don't have any visitors or friends, and why would they? They're a dull, retired couple with nothing better to do than cover a perfectly good house with blow-up toys and fairy lights."

Gerald's computer emitted a ringing noise.

"Now you'll have to go. This is an important call."

As Keya closed the study door behind her, despondent that she'd learned very little from her morning's interviews, Annie called from the doorway into the kitchen diner. "Don't forget your cake!"

She walked towards them and said, "I forgot to give you any earlier, as I was making Ryan his sandwich, but here's some for you both and a piece for Ryan when you see him later." She handed Keya four small foil-wrapped parcels. "And that one," she pointed to the largest, "is for your inspector."

Keya thanked Annie and, after she'd changed her shoes, she joined Warren outside and shivered. It hadn't warmed up, and, if anything, the wind was stronger.

"She's sweet on him!" said Warren, grinning.

"Sweet on who?" Keya asked in confusion. She'd thought that Annie was indifferent towards her husband.

"The inspector. Giving him the largest piece of cake."

"Cake. Yes. Oh! I see what you mean."

Warren was right. There had been a twinkle in Annie's eye when she'd spoken about Inspector Evans.

Shaking her head to clear the image of the inspector and Annie together, Keya said, "Now we'll speak to Gabrielle and Jackson, if they're at home."

CHAPTER TWENTY

As Keya stepped onto the drive of Gabrielle and Jackson's property, she heard a couple of sharp barks from Chief, Gabrielle's Treeing Walker Coonhound, inside the house. The breed was known for being alert, and Chief was clearly doing his job.

She was pleased to see that Gabrielle had listened to her. A brand-new wooden gate was propped against the gate post, and she wondered if Gabrielle was waiting for Larry's help to install it.

The security light clicked on as she and Warren approached the front door, and she pressed a modern-looking doorbell mounted on the wall. Chief's barking quietened down as they stood at the entrance.

Jackson's voice asked sullenly, "What do you want?"

"We need to ask you both some questions," Keya replied, feeling a little daft speaking to a box on a wall.

"Why?" asked Jackson.

But Keya heard Gabrielle say in the background, "Just let them in."

There was a buzzing noise, and the front door clicked open.

Keya looked at Warren, who grinned back at her. She pushed open the door and stepped inside. The decor was not dissimilar to the Becketts', with a cream, grey, and taupe colour scheme, but the messy hallway resembled Glenda's.

Chief bounded across the hardwood floor, tail wagging

enthusiastically. His nose immediately went to the floor, sniffing around Keya's shoes before darting to Warren, who knelt down to ruffle Chief's head.

Warren grinned and said, "Hello, Chief."

"You know my Chief!" Gabrielle declared in delight from the lounge. "He's such a sweetheart. Got him from a rescue center last year. He loves visitors."

Warren smiled awkwardly at Keya as they followed Chief into the lounge, where he promptly lay down by Gabrielle's feet, his eyes watchful and alert.

The lounge was furnished as Keya had expected it would be, with plush cream sofas, a myriad of scatter cushions, and a huge television screen attached to the wall.

She suspected Gabrielle was one of those people who became immune to the sound of the TV, as they always had it on in the background. But even with the sound turned down low, the bright images of dancing girls, which Warren was staring at, distracted Keya.

"Please can you turn that off?" she requested.

Gabrielle hunted around for the TV controls and eventually located them under a pile of glossy magazines.

"Well, don't stand there. Sit down and tell me all about your investigation into Gerald's death," Gabrielle urged them. "It's so exciting living next door to a potential murder victim. I've already asked my agent to pitch for me to host a show about it. I think I'd be great at true crime."

"Oh yes," Warren agreed enthusiastically.

Keya wasn't so sure, but she was more concerned about Gabrielle knowing that they had doubts about the cause of Gerald's death. She said, "Nobody has mentioned murder, Miss ...?"

"Please call me Gabrielle. Everyone does, and we're friends now, aren't we?"

"Oh yes," Warren repeated as he and Keya sat down on the sofa opposite Gabrielle.

Gabrielle smiled at him before returning her attention to Keya. Her eyes shone as she said, "A little birdie told me that Gerald's death might not be an accident."

"We don't know that, and besides, we haven't had the results of the post-mortem yet," Keya replied.

"You have," Gabrielle contested.

Keya's mouth fell open in surprise.

"She's right, Sarge. We have. I was supposed to tell you, but I forgot as you wanted to interview Mr Beckett." Warren looked down at his booted feet.

Gabrielle made a gagging sound.

"Are you all right?" asked Warren, looking up quickly.

"What a vile man. And he's so frightful to Annie. I've told her to leave him, and I'll find her a nice new man who will treat her properly. I know lots of single men who'd love someone like Annie to look after them."

Keya didn't disagree with Gabrielle's view of the Becketts, but she wanted to know more about the post-mortem.

"And?" said Keya, turning to Warren.

"And what?" Warren shrugged his shoulders.

"The result of the post-mortem."

"A heart attack as a result of being electrocuted," Gabrielle replied.

Which was just as Sujin had surmised, but how did Gabrielle know?

Keya narrowed her eyes at Gabrielle, who smiled back sweetly and then looked towards the door.

"Come in, darling," Gabrielle invited. "We were just talking about poor Gerald."

Keya considered that Gabrielle didn't appear to dislike or resent Gerald or his light display, but rather that she felt sorry for him.

"He might've had a moan to the council when our parties got a bit outta hand, but he wasn't a bad soul," Jackson said as he parked himself on the arm of Gabrielle's sofa. "He even helped me wire the video doorbell after we had trouble with someone leaving nasty notes for Gabrielle."

Keya wasn't aware of these, and she looked at Warren, who looked concerned, and she thought it was the first he'd heard about them, too.

"Did you report the harassment to the police?" Keya asked.

"No, I found out who it was and sorted him out meself."

Gabrielle shivered.

"Ye see," continued Jackson, "there is such a thing as bad publicity, and I try to protect Gabrielle as best I can."

Gabrielle stopped stroking Chief and placed her hand appreciatively on Jackson's leg.

"So you were friendly with Gerald?"

"I wouldn't say that," Jackson replied. "We were neighbours, and we had our disputes, but I had nothin' against him. And I certainly didn't mean him any harm. I like the lights, and the publicity hasn't been bad for Gabrielle either. A couple of photos of her in front of Gerald's house have gone viral online."

"How did Gerald feel about that?" asked Keya.

"I'd like to think he'd be chuffed, but who knows? He's dead," Jackson stated matter-of-factly.

Quite. So the photos had been taken, or at least had been shared after Gerald's death, Keya thought to herself. Out loud, she said, "We're trying to establish if Gerald had any enemies or anyone who'd want to harm him."

"So you do think he was murdered?" said Gabrielle breathlessly.

"No, but we have to rule it out before we present our findings to the coroner," Keya replied patiently. "Unless Gerald had a secret life we're not aware of …"

"Oh, that would be a great angle to pitch for my true crime show," interrupted Gabrielle.

Keya thought to herself that Gabrielle had forgotten that the first word was 'true,' not fantasy.

Jackson said, "The only people I ever saw him interact with were ourselves, Annie, and now and then her husband, but there was no love lost between him and Gerald, and Larry across the road. And we only saw him occasionally. The same can be said of Glenda."

Gabrielle looked disappointed. "Someone must have wanted him dead. He didn't electrocute himself."

As Keya and a reluctant Warren left Gabrielle and Jackson's house, Keya considered that she'd seen a different side of both the occupants.

They'd been far more level-headed and astute than when Keya had seen them before. And Jackson was less irritable and angry. And what about Gabrielle? There was certainly more to her than the face she put on for the public.

"What next?" asked Warren.

"I can't say we're any further forward than we were before we started this morning's interviews, except that we have learned there's a mole in either the station or the coroner's office. I haven't discovered anyone who had an issue with Gerald, and certainly nobody who had a reason to want him dead. Bartholomew Beckett is far more unpopular than Gerald ever was, so why didn't someone bump him off instead?"

CHAPTER TWENTY-ONE

"Sergeant, we're needed back at Limes Lane. Now."

Inspector Evans looked pained as he ran a hand through his thinning hair, combed over to hide his bald patch.

"Now?" Keya asked, surprised.

It was after half-past five, and she was tired and ready to go home after an afternoon spent typing up interview reports. At least staying at Zivah's meant she wouldn't have far to travel after finishing whatever task the inspector had for her. Still, why had he said we?

"And call Sujin. Ask him to meet us at the Sadlers' house," the inspector added.

"Oh no. Has something happened to Glenda?" Keya's mind raced. Surely, Glenda hadn't taken her own life?

"Not Glenda," the inspector replied evasively, striding out of the room. "I'll drive myself. You and Sujin make your own way there."

Keya picked up her phone and called Sujin.

"Hi," he answered. "Finished work?"

"I nearly had, but the inspector just rushed out and said he needs us at the Sadlers' house."

"Why?"

"I'm not sure. I asked if something had happened to Glenda, but he said it wasn't her, which makes it sound like someone else is involved. But I've no idea who or why."

"Probably a neighbourly dispute. Maybe someone got annoyed with people still visiting to see the lights. My money's on Jackson," Sujin speculated. "I bet he's punched someone."

Keya wasn't so sure. Before interviewing Jackson and Gabrielle, she would have agreed, but now?

"Let's stop guessing and get over there. Do you want me to drive you?" Keya asked.

"No thanks. I'd better take my car in case I need any of my equipment."

Keya shut down her computer, left the station, and drove back to Limes Lane.

Noticing flashing lights at the end of the street, she parked in Zivah and Aadi's drive and walked the rest of the way. An ambulance was parked outside Glenda's house. Warren was trying to keep the crowd at bay, but people kept pushing forward, phones raised, recording the scene.

She wondered if they re-watched the footage later or if they were hoping for a viral clip to make them famous for five seconds.

Keya pressed her lips together, thinking, as she made her way through the crowd.

"Hey! We were here first," a man complained.

"Police," Keya replied automatically.

She reached the ambulance, where one of the green-clad crew was leaning against the passenger door.

"Sergeant Varma," Keya introduced herself, hoping the woman wouldn't ask for her warrant card.

"They're over there," the woman replied in a bored tone, gesturing towards Glenda's property, near the fence separating it from the Becketts'.

Keya picked her way across the garden, taking care not to trip over an inflatable decoration, until she reached the inspector and another paramedic.

To the side, Glenda and Annie were comforting each other, their faces hidden in the shadows.

"A rum business," the inspector muttered as he looked across at Keya.

She glanced around, trying to see what he meant. At first, all she saw was the giant inflatable Father Christmas which had been climbing up the side of the house. Then she noticed an arm and a leg sticking out from under it.

"Who is that?" she asked.

"It's Bart," Annie called back. "He'd been complaining about that Santa all afternoon. I told him I'd spoken to Glenda, and we'd agreed to ask Larry to take it, and some of the other decorations, down, but he wouldn't listen."

"Is he...?" Keya looked at the paramedic, who nodded.

"I checked his pulse as soon as I got here, but there wasn't one. I made sure not to move him so the scene wouldn't be disturbed. I figured you'd want to investigate. How long until your crime scene technician arrives?"

"I'm here," Sujin called, slightly breathless as he lifted a black bag over an illuminated snowboarding owl with a red and white scarf.

"Right, I'll give you my verbal report and be on my way," said the paramedic. "There's no point in hanging around. Although that crowd might cause another accident if they don't clear off. I don't envy your constable."

Keya glanced towards the ambulance and saw the flashing lights of several phones still recording.

"So, what do we have?" asked Sujin.

"One moment," the inspector said, standing next to a ladder leaning against the house. "Sergeant, escort the ladies inside."

"Of course," Keya replied. She carefully made her way past the large Santa, keeping close to the fence. When she reached Annie and Glenda, she said, "Let's leave them to it. Do you have a back door?"

Glenda nodded, and with one last glance at the prone Santa, led Keya and Annie to the rear of the house.

It was a relief to walk along a clear gravel path, free of decorations and flashing lights.

Inside, Keya found the rear utility area as untidy as the hallway had been during her previous visit.

A plastic laundry basket sat on top of the washing machine, with a pair of jeans draped over the side. Unlike Annie's house, there was no shoe rack, and boots and shoes were piled haphazardly in a corner.

Glenda sat at the dining table as Annie switched on the kettle. The two women seemed comfortable together, with Annie clearly familiar with the layout of Glenda's kitchen.

"I'm sorry to make you go over this, but I need to take your statements to work out how Bartholomew died."

"Of course," Annie said, wiping a splash of milk off the worktop.

"You know Bart's views on Gerald's lights. He was always saying they lowered the tone of the area. He threatened to do something about them, and even after Gerald died, he kept complaining. But this afternoon, he was furious about that giant Santa. He said he couldn't concentrate on his work. I don't know why he became so obsessed with it all of a sudden."

Keya wondered guiltily if it was because she had pointed it out.

From the table, Glenda said in a small voice, "I was going to take them down. When I had the energy."

"This isn't your fault," Annie insisted.

Keya heard a knock, and Gabrielle walked in through the back door and declared, "Bart only has himself to blame." Her blonde hair was tied in an untidy bun, and she wore minimal makeup, which made her look younger and more vulnerable.

"What happened?" Keya asked.

"I'm not sure," Annie said as she opened a cupboard above the kettle. "I was at home."

"And I was with her," Glenda said unexpectedly.

Annie knocked a red mug off the counter. "Sorry," she said in a shaky voice, leaning down to pick up the broken pieces.

"Don't worry," Glenda said. "I've plenty more. You might want the white milk jug from the top shelf."

Annie continued making the tea, and as she reached for the milk jug, Keya picked up the broken pieces from the floor. Among them was a larger green fragment. It looked like a spout and was not part of the broken cup.

Keya placed the pieces on the counter and said, "I know this isn't easy."

Annie said nothing as she poured the tea.

Gabrielle answered Keya's earlier question, "Annie and Glenda were having tea at Annie's, weren't you?" She looked at the pair.

"Yes, we were," Glenda agreed, her voice stronger. "Annie's always trying to cheer me up." As if to confirm, Annie poured hot water into a green teapot.

"And where were you?" Keya asked Gabrielle, seeing she was the most willing to talk.

"At home. I came over when I heard a cry."

"From whom?"

"Bart, I presume."

Annie placed the milk jug on the table, handing cups of tea to Gabrielle and Keya.

"I didn't hear Bart go out," Annie said. "Did you, Glenda?"

"No," Glenda replied, looking serious.

"Do you know where he got the ladder from?" Keya asked.

"It was Gerald's," Glenda explained. "He always left it lying around. Never cared about security." She gave a forced laugh. "I think it was propped up against the garage."

"So, Bart found the ladder and carried it round to the side of the house?" Keya prompted, aware that she was leading the witnesses but unsure how else to get the information. "Then he climbed up to take down the Santa... and fell off?"

"Yes," Glenda and Gabrielle said together.

More hesitantly, Annie added, "I guess he must have."

"It's OK," Keya said, placing her cup down and gently guiding Annie to a chair.

As she sat down, Glenda reached out and took Annie's hand, squeezing it.

"So what happened next?" Keya asked.

"We all walked around the house together and that's when we saw him. Bart, lying on the ground," Gabrielle said.

"Under the Santa," Glenda added quickly.

"Did you try to help him?"

"We had to turn off the electricity," Glenda said, her lip quivering. "After what happened to Gerald…"

"Jackson did that," Gabrielle added.

"And what did you do when it was safe?" Keya asked.

"We checked his pulse, but there wasn't one," Gabrielle replied.

"I tried talking to him, but he didn't respond," sniffed Annie.

Gabrielle added, "So I called an ambulance."

CHAPTER TWENTY-TWO

Keya was in Glenda's kitchen, trying to piece together what had happened to Bartholomew Beckett, when she heard Inspector Evans call, "Hello?"

"We're in the kitchen, sir." Keya sipped her tea and glanced around at the other women. Glenda and Annie sat quietly at the dining table, their heads bowed. Keya wondered what they were thinking.

The lead-up to Christmas was usually joyful, but these two women would be arranging funerals rather than celebrations.

The inspector appeared in the kitchen doorway, a pained expression on his face. His gaze fell on Annie, who looked up, and he gave her a small, understanding smile. After all, it hadn't been that long since he had lost his mother, to whom he'd been very close.

Nodding, he turned his attention to Keya. "Sergeant, can you help Sujin? Constable Sparrow has his hands full with the crowd of onlookers, which is swelling since news of a second death got out." The inspector glanced quickly at Annie and Glenda.

"Of course." Keya took a final sip of tea. She looked once more at Glenda, Annie, and Gabrielle, who was engrossed in her phone, before leaving the kitchen.

The study door was open, and Keya stepped inside. An empty box that had contained the inflatable elf was discarded next to the wastepaper basket. She picked it up but found nothing more sinister than an empty box.

Returning it to the floor, she noticed several piles of coins and a few five-pound notes on the table. It struck her as odd that Gerald would use cash for his decorations; surely he'd have bought them online with a credit card. Perhaps this was just loose change left lying around.

Outside, she found Sujin where she'd left him, with the now deflated giant Santa. He was examining Bartholomew's body in situ.

"How can I help?" asked Keya.

"Is it worth putting up a cordon?" Sujin asked.

"I should do that, and you'll want me decked out in one of your paper suits, I presume?"

"Gloves and shoe covers will be enough. I'll process the scene around the body. No point bothering with DNA beyond that, given how many people have come and gone. I'd be more suspicious if there wasn't any evidence of Mrs. Sadler or her neighbours."

Keya noticed that Sujin had sensibly parked in Glenda's driveway, sparing him the ordeal of pushing through the crowd outside the front gate. She could just make out Ryan's voice, along with Warren's, trying to keep the crowd under control.

She felt self-conscious as several phone lights turned in her direction, filming her movements. Pulling on latex gloves and covering her shoes, she collected evidence bags and a roll of police tape.

The outer cordon along the front fence, put up after Gerald's death, was still there, as was the inner cordon where Gerald's body had been found. Keya created a second inner cordon, attaching the "Police Line Do Not Cross" tape to a drainpipe, wrapping it around a small tree, and securing it to a nail sticking out of the house wall.

She helped Sujin wrestle the deflated Santa into a large evidence bag and placed several strings of lights into other bags.

Sujin returned to the body, his face illuminated in the dim light, and frowned.

"What's wrong?" Keya asked.

"The victim is wearing slippers."

"That makes sense. The wives said he was working at home. They didn't even realize he was missing until they heard a cry and found him out here."

"But the slippers are very clean."

"Again, not surprising. He was fastidious about everything being in the right place. I can't imagine him with an old, scuffed, or fraying pair of slippers."

"Hmm," was Sujin's only response.

Keya continued her search of the garden but found little of interest. They couldn't take all the garden decorations back to the station. She wondered if Glenda would now ask Larry to take them down. After all, they had been the cause of two deaths.

Standing up, Keya glanced through a side window into the kitchen-diner. Inside, she saw Inspector Evans giving Annie a hug. She winced, hoping he wouldn't crush her fragile frame.

She considered how much more—what was the right word?—human the inspector had become since his mother's death. He would never have shown grieving relatives such empathy or support in the past.

"Evening," said a voice Keya didn't recognise. She turned to see a new green-clad ambulance worker. "I'm from the coroner's office."

Keya carried the evidence bags back to Sujin's car while he and the ambulance staff organised the removal of Bartholomew's body.

"Hey, you can't go in there!" she heard Ryan call as a shadowy figure, holding up a phone with a bright light, entered the garden.

Still wearing her gloves and shoe covers, Keya shut the car door and ran across the garden to intercept the intruder.

"Oh, toda!" she exclaimed as she tripped over the illuminated entrance to a polystyrene igloo. Despite landing flat on her face, she refrained from swearing. Taking a deep breath, she pushed herself into a kneeling position, shading her eyes from the bright light now aimed at her.

"I'll take that," said Ryan, grabbing the phone.

"Hey! Give that back!" shouted the intruder.

"As you deliberately crossed a police cordon and ignored my request to return, this phone is now evidence. If you give me your name and address, I'll return it after considering whether to charge you with interfering in a police investigation."

"Well, I…"

The exchange gave Keya time to get to her feet. Rubbing her left arm, she said, "Perhaps we should just delete tonight's footage and give the phone back. I'm not sure we have time to waste on people with nothing better to do than film someone else's trauma. It sickens me."

She looked past Ryan at the other phone lights trained on her. "You should all feel ashamed of yourselves. Two families have lost loved ones just before Christmas, and you're trying to profit from their grief. Where's your compassion?"

Several lights flicked off, and Keya heard muttering in the crowd.

Ryan handed the phone back to the intruder and said, "I'd prefer to keep this, but as my colleague said, we have better things to do. I've deleted everything from tonight. Now go home and find something useful to do rather than hanging around crime scenes. It's morbid."

The young man snatched his phone, and to Keya's surprise, the crowd jeered at him, even though they were equally guilty.

"You OK?" Ryan asked as Keya peeled off her gloves.

"Yes. I knew this garden would be a hazard, and I've been careful all evening." She rubbed her shoulder. It did ache.

"I think your lecture worked," Ryan noted.

Only one phone light remained on, and the crowd's murmuring had quieted.

"Water and cold drinks, only a pound!" shouted Larry's familiar voice. "Or try my honey or my chilli jam!"

Ryan smiled. "Hopefully Larry's hawking will clear the rest of them out."

They watched solemnly as the two ambulance crew members carried a stretcher through the garden with more dexterity than Keya could have managed. Laid on it was a black bag containing Bartholomew Beckett's body.

Sujin joined them. "Body number two," he said ruefully. "Let's hope it's the last on this street." Then, turning to Ryan, he said, "Can you help me with the ladder?"

Perhaps Sujin did want to take it back to the station.

As Ryan and Sujin moved to handle the ladder, Keya said, "While you do that, I'll have a word with Larry."

CHAPTER TWENTY-THREE

M ost of the remaining crowd dispersed with the departure of the ambulance, and Keya strode across Limes Lane to join Warren and Larry.

"Here you go, son. Collect the rubbish before it blows away," Larry said, holding out a black dustbin bag.

Warren gave Keya a 'do-I-have-to?' look, and she nodded.

Grabbing the bag from Larry, Warren sloped off.

"I should ask if you have a licence to sell these, Larry, now that I'm working in a semi-official capacity," Keya said, "but let's just say that tonight is the last night you're open for business."

"Really?" Larry looked disappointed.

"I think Glenda's going to ask you to take down the lights anyway. They've caused enough trouble."

"Aye, well, that's true."

Keya waited for Larry to ask about Bartholomew, and when he didn't, she said, "I thought you'd be curious to know what happened to your neighbour."

"He fell off Gerald's ladder, the stupid idiot. What did he think he was doing? Overweight and unfit, and I don't think he had a clue about electrics. If he hadn't toppled off, he'd probably have electrocuted himself. That's why I had to turn the power off before anyone touched him to check if he was OK."

"You were there?" None of the wives had mentioned Larry's presence.

"Oh, yeah, well, I saw them all in the garden. Glenda, Annie, Gabrielle, and Jackson, so I went to see what was going on."

"And that's when you saw Bart's body?"

"Yes, I mean no. Part of it from under that huge Santa he brought down with him."

"And then you, not Jackson, turned off the power?"

"I suggested it, after what happened to Gerald, but it might have been Jackson who actually turned off the electricity at the fuse box inside the front door. I can't remember."

Keya let the point go and looked across at his stall, which had an open cool box containing cans of drink resting beside it. "How have your sales been?" she asked, feeling the need to move away from the subject of Bartholomew's death.

"Good enough to pay for some groceries for the next few weeks, and my heating bill."

It couldn't be easy for older people on fixed pension incomes, Keya reflected, especially with the increase in energy costs during the winter. No wonder Larry wanted to raise some extra cash to help him get by.

Cash. She thought of the piles on Gerald's desk and then asked, "Was it just a slow start last week?"

"Must have been or, as I suspected, folk weren't as honest as I'd hoped. But I've made up for the shortfall, so I can't complain."

Across at Glenda's house, Inspector Evans stepped out of the front door. He turned and said something to whoever was inside.

"I should offer to take the decorations down rather than wait for Glenda to ask me," Larry said. "And see if she or Annie need anything doing now their husbands are no longer with us. Not that they were much practical use when they were alive."

Larry walked across the road and met Inspector Evans on Glenda's garden path.

As soon as Larry passed him, Warren scuttled back to Keya and said, "Can I finish now and go home? My tea will be cold, again."

Keya was so used to working long hours, especially when there was a major crime to investigate, that she sometimes forgot that her younger and less senior colleagues also had other duties at the station. How long had Warren been working today?

"Of course, sorry."

Warren thrust the rubbish bag into her hand and recrossed the road before she had a chance to protest.

She was wondering what to do with the rubbish when she saw Ryan and Sujin walk round the side of the house, without a ladder.

When Sujin stopped to speak to the inspector, Larry nodded, said something to Ryan, and then continued up the garden path to Glenda's front door. Ryan walked in the opposite direction and joined Keya, who was still standing beside Larry's stall.

"Have you really been collecting rubbish?" he asked, eyeing the dustbin bag.

"No, Warren did it, grudgingly. Do you think we've finished?"

"It looks like it. The body's been transported to the mortuary, and Sujin's finished examining the ladder. We decided it wasn't something we wanted in the station during the lead-up to Christmas. Too much temptation for police officers, never mind those who are arrested over the festive period."

"And?" Keya asked.

"And what did Sujin find? I've no idea. He muttered to himself, but I can't see this being anything other than an unfortunate accident. What did Mr. Beckett think he was doing climbing that ladder?" Ryan's comments mirrored Larry's thoughts, it seemed.

Keya looked at Ryan and remembered where he'd been that afternoon. "Sorry, this wasn't what you needed this evening. How was your interview?"

Ryan grinned. "Really good." Then he looked uncertain. "I shouldn't say that, should I? In case I jinx it."

"I don't know. Did you see any other candidates there?"

"Yes, but then there are several positions with this organisation, which is good. It gives me a better chance, especially as they said the hard bit is reaching the interview stage."

"So, can you share what it is?" Keya asked, unable to hide her curiosity and irritation at not knowing.

Ryan looked at her, drawing his eyebrows together as he apologised, "I'm really sorry, but I can't. Not yet."

Gritting her teeth in frustration, she watched Sujin and Inspector Evans cross the road to join them.

"Is it a coincidence that we have two unexplained deaths in the same location within a week of each other?" Inspector Evans looked at Sujin.

"I think so. I'll re-examine the evidence from the first case, and there are a couple of points I need to clear up with this one. And, of course, we have to wait for the results of the post-mortem."

"I'd like both cases wrapped up and handed over to the coroner by the end of the week," the inspector announced. "Anything we can do to improve our position, and our clear-up rate, in the eyes of the chief constable is worth doing."

Keya presumed he was referring to the station review. But would these cases make any difference to whether or not their team was disbanded?

CHAPTER TWENTY-FOUR

K eya started Tuesday morning at the café by checking the upcoming week's menu with Monica and Mick.

Sitting at a table close to Norman's hot drinks counter, Mick asked, "Can you look at the Christmas pie I made yesterday?"

Keya wasn't sure whether a Christmas pie was sweet or savoury, but she felt delighted, and a little guilty, that Mick had spent his day off cooking prospective dishes for the café.

She knew how much he enjoyed and valued his job after the years he'd spent in prison, but that he also wanted to travel and experience the world.

While Mick returned to the kitchen, Keya turned in her chair and looked up at Norman, who was placing a deluxe Christmas hot chocolate on a tray. She'd seen a recipe on Sunday in the food section of the paper, which she'd amended and upgraded.

Norman was to add a pinch of nutmeg and half a teaspoon of ground cinnamon to the milk in the frothing jug, along with a couple of slices of orange, peel included. The idea was that as the milk heated up, the flavours would infuse into it.

The slices of orange were to be removed from the hot chocolate before serving, but a piece of Terry's chocolate orange was to be pushed into the thick whipped cream squirted on top of the drink instead of a chocolate flake.

She also wanted to sprinkle candied orange over it, but so far, she'd only found tubs containing large pieces that were too time-consuming and difficult to chop finely.

When Millie had carried the tray away, Keya asked Norman, "Have you cleared up the planning consent conditions on the barn at Meadowbank Farm?"

Norman shook his head regretfully. "Useless. We had a meeting with the assistant planning officer, but he just scratched his head and said he wasn't sure of the exact meaning. There's one more planning committee meeting before Christmas, so he's putting the consent back to them to clarify. Why he let it be issued like that, I've no idea."

"So you still don't know if Dotty will be able to open her antique shop?"

"No, and I'm concerned that she won't. But we have neither the energy nor the money to continue fighting the council on it."

"Here you are," Mick said, placing a white side plate on the counter in front of Norman. "My Christmas pie."

Mick carried a tray across to Keya's table, which held several more side plates of pie, along with knives and forks.

Keya picked up a plate. The pie was savoury, with a central layer of chicken or turkey between two layers of sausage meat, all enclosed in crisp pastry.

Not wanting to actually eat the meat, Keya lifted the plate to her nose and sniffed. There was sage and thyme, and a hint of nutmeg. And were those cranberries in the sausage meat?

"Millie," Mick called, and she joined them at the table.

"Apricots," Millie said, tasting a piece of pie.

"And chestnuts?" queried Monica.

"Yes," Mick replied, glancing uncertainly from Monica to Millie.

"This is good," muttered Norman through a mouthful of pie.

"Will you serve it hot or cold?" Keya asked.

"Cold, with a crunchy Christmas slaw, which includes red cabbage," Mick answered.

"Oh, that sounds good," Keya replied. "Shall we serve that instead of a normal coleslaw during the festive period?"

"It would make it easier," Monica agreed. "And it will add some lovely colour to the dishes."

"Excellent, Mick. We'll serve that once we've finished the pork and chicken terrine."

Millie's phone pinged, and she placed her plate of half-eaten pie on the table before stepping away.

"Any other menu suggestions?" Keya asked.

"Not as such," replied Monica. "But Alison and Millie have started receiving requests from customers about ordering food for Christmas. Is it something you've considered?"

"I haven't," Keya replied, wondering why the idea hadn't occurred to her. "What are they asking for?"

"Mince pies, Christmas puddings, and Christmas cakes. Aunt Beanie said her husband enjoyed his festive afternoon tea so much, she wondered if she could order another to take to him this week?"

"Would you be able to do that?"

Monica looked at Mick, who nodded. "With a day's notice. But ..." Monica trailed off.

"Is something wrong?" Keya asked in a concerned voice.

"Would you mind if Maitri helped us?" Monica asked. "She says she's bored in the deli and would love to help us in the kitchen."

"Really? I didn't think she was interested in cooking."

"I think it's more the serving and customer side. But there's plenty she can do while Mick and I concentrate on preparing the food."

"OK, I'll speak to her, but what do we do about the deli if she's busy in the kitchen?" Keya said out loud, but it was a question she needed to answer herself.

Millie returned to the table and shuffled from one foot to another.

Keya looked up at her with a quizzical expression.

"I know it's rather short notice, but can I have tomorrow off?"

"I don't see why not. I'll ask Zivah if she can cover. Doing anything nice? Christmas shopping in London or Bristol?"

Pink patches appeared on Millie's cheeks, but she replied, "Nothing like that. But there is somewhere I'd like to visit before Christmas."

Keya wondered where, but she didn't push it. "I'm sure that'll be fine." She pushed her chair back and said, "Well done, everyone. Great effort and some wonderful ideas. I'll go and talk to Maitri about helping out in the kitchen."

Keya left the café by the patio doors, stepping outside into the chill winter weather. She felt a raindrop and hurried past the wooden-framed outdoor seating area. As she entered the single-storey deli, the rain started in earnest.

Maitri was leaning against the counter, reading a booklet which was open in front of her.

"Are you so bored you've resorted to reading magazines?" Keya asked, only half joking.

"Actually, it's a prospectus for the University of the West of England."

"Oh," Keya responded in surprise. "I didn't think you wanted to go to uni? That you preferred to learn while working."

"I do, but Millie told me about apprenticeships, and UWE has partnered up with some larger retailers to provide them. There's one here working for a supermarket chain where I'd also get a degree, which they would pay for, and I have the potential to earn over £40,000 by the end of the four-year apprenticeship."

"Wow, maybe I should do that," but Keya knew, even if the salary was tempting, she had enough on her plate.

Maitri turned over the page. "Or I could do a shorter hospitality supervisor course, with hands-on training, and the opportunity of an in-house apprenticeship with a hotel chain after I've finished."

"They both sound like interesting options," Keya said, realising she was relieved that her youngest sister was looking to continue her education and experience. She'd started to worry and feel responsible for her over the past few months as the deli had become quieter.

"And Monica suggested that while you're not busy here, you could help out in the kitchen."

Maitri's face brightened. "Would that be OK? I mean, not necessarily cooking, but making sandwiches, and preparing the plates for serving and …"

"That's fine," Keya cut in. "But what about the deli stock?"

They both looked around at the stacked shelves.

"We could sell some in the café like we used to," Keya suggested, answering her own question.

"And what about Christmas hampers?" Maitri suggested. "Are you going to let people order food from the café?"

"Christmas cakes and mince pies? Yes, I think so."

"Then we could offer them alongside deli items to create hampers, which I can display in the café."

"Good idea. And I could ask Gilly if we can sell any we have left in the reception area at the Christmas auctions she's planning, and perhaps we could enter a larger hamper in the actual auction?"

"Oh, yes," said Maitri, sounding enthusiastic again. It was her energy and positivity that had made the deli such a success over the summer.

Feeling happier, Keya braced herself against the rain and ran back to the café, throwing open the patio doors and entering breathlessly without getting too wet.

"It's nasty out there," said Norman when she approached his drinks counter. "Can you try one of the Christmas hot chocolates and check I've got the spices right?"

Keya smiled. "That sounds like a delicious idea."

CHAPTER TWENTY-FIVE

Keya grabbed a takeaway sandwich from the café after a reasonable lunchtime trade and drove to Cirencester police station. As she entered her team room, Stan and Ryan abruptly ceased their conversation.

"Am I interrupting?" Keya asked in a concerned tone. Had she missed an announcement about the station?

"No, it's nothing to worry about. Ryan and I ..." Stan trailed off. He was standing in front of Ryan's desk.

"Oh, I see." Keya placed her hands on her hips. "It's about your new job. So it's OK for Stan to know?" She knew she sounded petulant, but she'd always supported Ryan and considered him a friend. She didn't understand why he refused to tell her about his potential new role.

"It's not like that," Ryan protested, looking up from his chair behind his desk. "I've been asked back for a day of assessments, and I'm not sure how much I'm allowed to tell you." He looked up at Stan.

Stan shrugged his shoulders.

"And Stan helped me with my application while you were off sick."

"Not that sick," Keya said, although her left shoulder did ache after her fall the previous evening. Perhaps she should book an appointment with the doctor to check it out.

"Besides," Ryan continued, "I'm applying for an intelligence job, so I expect the assessment will be more data-driven."

"Which is why I was telling him that I'm as much use as a chocolate teapot," Stan admitted. "And talking of tea, anyone fancy a cuppa?"

"I'd love one," Keya replied. "And I mustn't forget to eat my sandwich." She sat down at her desk and switched on her computer, feeling guilty about her earlier outburst. She wondered what had brought it on.

Ryan interrupted her thoughts. "Thank you for giving Millie the day off tomorrow to visit the university in Bristol. She and Maitri seem really excited about applying for apprenticeship positions."

Keya caught herself and was relieved that her face was hidden behind her computer monitor. She tried processing what Ryan had just said in the context of her earlier discussions with Millie and Maitri at the café.

Maitri had been looking through a university prospectus. Was it for the one in Bristol which Millie was visiting tomorrow?

Keya said in a neutral tone, "Maitri told me that during the courses, you get to work with top retail companies."

Stan returned, carrying mugs of tea.

"Oh, yes. With the one Millie is interested in, she'll be employed by an international supermarket chain and given days off to study at university. And the salary is good, with guaranteed increases if she completes certain steps in the course."

Which would mean, Keya reasoned, Millie leaving the café. She took her mug of tea from Stan and sat back, considering this latest piece of information.

Stan smiled ruefully at her and said, "Do you ever get that feeling you're being left behind?"

She stared up at him. "Yes, I do, and that so much is happening, and it's completely out of my control."

Stan nodded. "It's disconcerting, isn't it? And change is never easy to deal with. It unsettles people."

He was right. She was feeling … what was that big word people sometimes used? Discombobulated.

"That's right, Stan. I feel discombobulated."

"Dear me," commiserated Inspector Evans as he walked into the team room. "I hope it's not contagious."

"Like the changes everyone's contemplating for their lives?" she responded in a sardonic voice, staring up at her boss.

She was surprised to see his face colour. So he was hiding something.

In an attempt to cover up his discomfort, the inspector said, "Sujin thinks he's found something interesting about the plug Gerald Sadler connected his faulty Christmas decoration to. Why don't you see what it is? I need to make some calls."

Keya eyed her untouched sandwich and her half-drunk mug of tea. Picking the tea up, she left the team room, wondering if the inspector's calls were official business or of a more personal nature.

Stan was right. She found the uncertainty of change disconcerting.

Carrying her mug, she entered the custody area of the station, where Sujin had his office. Three uniformed constables were standing with two men and a woman in their thirties in front of the custody desk.

The men were still wearing paper party hats, and the string from a party popper hung from the woman's sleeve.

"I told you not to tell him we were together," the woman slurred at one of the men. The second man turned angrily and raised a fist but was quickly restrained by an officer.

"Christmas parties," muttered the duty sergeant as he passed Keya. When he reached the group, he said, "Right, what do we have here?"

Christmas tunes were permeating through Sujin's closed workroom door. She knocked and entered.

"Hi," Sujin said, smiling up at her and turning down the festive music. "I'm glad you're here. Both the inspector and Ryan seem preoccupied, and this isn't something I want to entrust to Warren."

"What have you discovered?" Keya asked.

"I re-examined all the items we brought back from the Sadlers' after Gerald's death, and I found a piece of down trapped in the hinge of the cover for the outdoor plug."

Sujin turned and picked up a circular Petri dish, which reminded Keya of her school science lessons. Inside it was something white and fluffy.

"It looks like a feather?"

"Down is the smallest, finest feather found closest to a duck's or goose's skin. Young chicks are covered in it before their feathers develop."

"How did it get on the plug?" Keya asked. "The Sadlers didn't keep any birds, not even chickens. In fact, they had no pets."

Sujin looked up at Keya, a rueful expression on his face.

"You want me to find out?" Keya questioned.

Sujin nodded.

"But you want me to tread carefully, and not upset the residents of Limes Lane or give them any indication that we're continuing to look at Gerald's death as potentially suspicious?"

"You've got it. I knew you were the right officer for the job."

"And here I was, hoping for a quiet afternoon to write out my reports and eat my lunch."

"At three o'clock?"

"Exactly!"

CHAPTER TWENTY-SIX

K eya ate her sandwich as she drove to Limes Lane. She knew she shouldn't eat while driving, but she snatched mouthfuls when she stopped at traffic lights or queued at junctions.

Her shoulder was still aching. She really must make an appointment to see the doctor.

All was quiet on Limes Lane, and when she parked in front of Glenda's house, she was relieved to see Larry taking down Christmas decorations. Annie was standing on a small set of steps, unwrapping fairy lights from around a bush.

Keya wasn't sure how much evidence she'd be able to collect since the inner cordon tape around the area where Gerald's body had been found had either snapped or been cut. It was clear that either Larry, Glenda, or Annie had entered it to remove more decorations.

As Keya opened the garden gate and walked up the front path, Glenda emerged from the house carrying a cardboard box. "I've found the one for the snowman," she told Larry.

A phone rang, and Annie let the fairy lights fall as she answered the call. "Hi," she said nervously.

Keya continued walking.

"It doesn't give me much time," said Annie anxiously.

"Back again," Larry said, looking up and spotting Keya.

"I'm afraid so. I've been asked to check something," Keya replied.

"Do you really think I can?" Annie asked her unknown caller.

"Oh?" Larry stood up.

"Have any of you ever kept ducks or geese?" Keya asked.

"OK, if you're certain this is allowed. But I need to think about it," Annie said.

Keya realised she was being distracted by Annie's call. What uncertainty and change had her husband's death triggered for her? And for Glenda?

"Now, I used to keep geese," Larry remarked, taking the box from Glenda. "Vicious they were, but I made some good money at Christmas. You do know that goose used to be the bird of choice for all the winter festivals because they were ready to eat at this time of year?"

"No, I didn't," Keya admitted.

"But I gave up keeping them after they attacked a door-to-door salesman. I argued they were for security purposes, but the local council didn't see it that way."

Larry smiled ruefully. "But nobody around here breeds geese anymore. And as for ducks, you might find some on the pond beyond the wood."

"But you haven't seen any round here?" Keya pressed.

"Na," Larry said, turning his attention back to the deflated snowman, which he started pushing into the empty box. "And I ain't likely to."

Annie had finished her call and was unwrapping the final section of fairy lights. Climbing carefully down the steps, she carried the lights across and asked Larry, "Where shall I put these?"

"Hello," Keya said.

"Hi," Annie replied, not looking at Keya.

Keya wondered if she'd done something wrong. It wasn't like Annie to ignore her, but then, as she'd considered only a few minutes earlier, Annie had just lost her husband. However rude and unpalatable Keya thought he'd been, she presumed Annie had still loved him.

As Annie lifted the lights, Keya noticed a rip in her jacket and the white filling that poked out of it. Of course, goose and duck down were used as insulation.

"Shall I take those?" Keya offered. She reached forward, brushing against Annie's sleeve and the rip on it. She pinched at the filling as she did so.

"Thank you," Annie said gratefully, handing the lights to Keya. "Do you mind if I go home?"

"Of course not, and thank you for your help," Glenda responded, sounding more confident and self-assured than she had since her husband's death.

Annie nodded and, with her head bowed, walked down the garden path.

"Is she all right?" Keya asked.

"Not really. She doesn't know what to do now Bart is dead. It's a lot to think about, believe me," replied Glenda as she took the fairy lights from Keya and placed them in another box.

"I'm not sure what I'll do with all these. I won't be decorating the house next year, and after what happened to Gerald, I daren't sell them."

As Glenda discussed what to do with the lights and inflatable decorations, Keya turned away and placed several small feathers, which she'd snagged from Annie's jacket, in a small transparent evidence bag. It was one of several she'd remembered to bring with her.

She'd take what she'd found back to Sujin, although she couldn't think why Annie would have wanted to harm Glenda's husband when she had her hands full with her own. She doubted Annie had the knowledge to tamper with the electronic control box.

Mind you, Annie was intelligent, and she might have picked up the box and thought that swapping the wires around would stop the lights from working, without considering the fatal effect her meddling might have.

"How about a break and a cup of tea with a slice of cake?" suggested Glenda. "I have so much food since considerate people like Annie, Gabrielle, and the ladies from the church keep dropping items off for me."

"I wouldn't say no," Larry replied. "And it might help me work out how to take down the reindeer and sleigh from the roof. How did Gerald get them up there?"

"I've no idea," admitted Glenda. "But you're not to start climbing up to get them. Why don't you ask Ryan to help you take them down?"

"Aye, that's a grand idea. Now let's have that cake."

As Keya had the potential source of the feathers, she knew she should return to the station, but she was intrigued by the change in Glenda and her new openness. Perhaps she would learn more about Gerald. And she didn't want to give up the offer of a cup of tea.

Keya followed Larry inside the house and immediately noticed a change. The hallway was clear of clutter, and a tall brown cardboard box with a removal company's name on the side stood against one wall. The end of a green knitted scarf was hanging over the side of it.

Glenda and Larry stopped beside the box, and Glenda said, "Help yourself to anything you want. The rest I'll take to a charity shop."

Keya glanced into the workroom, which had also been cleared of empty boxes. The toolbox was still on the table, but its lid had been closed and the table was clear, apart from an empty cup, a pottery dish, and the two piles of money.

Thinking about the money, Keya entered the kitchen and said, "I see you've cleared up Gerald's study."

"I had to start sometime, and that seemed as good a place as any to begin," Glenda replied as she filled the kettle with water from the tap.

"But those piles of money bother me. It seems out of character for Gerald to have them," Keya remarked.

"You mean Gerald would have left bits of change lying around all over the place?"

"Yes, I suppose I do."

"Then you'd be right. Recently he'd hardly used cash at all, buying most of his decorations with his credit card. He said it was easier to return them if they were faulty."

"So where did the money come from?"

"I've no idea. I only noticed it after Gerald's death, and it wasn't there the last time I tried to clean his workroom, which would have been the weekend before he died."

"Do you know how much there is?" Keya asked.

"No idea," replied Glenda, turning her attention back to preparing tea.

Unsure why the money bothered her, Keya returned to the study and gathered it up, placing one pile in the empty mug and the other in the dish.

Larry was sitting at the dining table, so Keya sat opposite him and tipped the money out of the cup. "Can you count that, and I'll do the same for this?" She tipped over the dish.

"All right, but I'm not sure why? There are plenty of pieces round here Glenda could sell if you're worried about her supporting herself. And I'm sure she'll benefit from Gerald's pension."

Which was a good point, Keya considered as she started counting her pile of coins. When she'd finished and added the three five-pound notes to the total, she said, "That's forty-seven pounds, sixty-five pence and a button. I'm not sure where the button came from."

"You'd be amazed what people put in my honesty box. Buttons, badges, plastic toys, and I even had a handwritten IOU, but I doubt whoever put that in will come back and pay what they owe me."

Glenda placed a tray on the table and sat down.

As she poured tea from a green teapot, Keya asked Larry, "How much do you have?"

"Fifty-six pounds and eight pence."

"Larry's right. Those aren't large sums. I should probably donate them to the church. Annie's asked me to go with her to the Christingle service on Sunday afternoon."

"That's nice," Keya replied, although she had no idea what a Christingle service was.

"Hang on a minute," said Larry, staring at the coins and ignoring the slice of fruitcake Glenda had placed next to him. "Around fifty pounds is the amount I reckon I was short from my honesty box on Monday and Tuesday last week. You don't think Gerald stole the money, do you?"

Glenda sipped her tea, her elbows resting on the table. She said with a note of disgust in her voice, "It wouldn't surprise me, although to think Gerald would stoop so low. He was annoyed about your stall and complained that you were profiting from his work. I pointed out that you had to put up with all the visitors coming to see his decorations, so it was only fair you should make a few pounds out of it. But I could tell he wasn't appeased by that."

"You had no idea he was the one taking the money?" Keya asked suddenly suspicious. Theft was a motive, if not for murder, at least to tamper with Gerald's lights.

"It never crossed my mind." Larry shook his head. "I didn't think Gerald was that petty." Larry broke up his fruitcake and picked up a bitesize piece.

"Oh, if he got something into his head," remarked Glenda, "there was no talking him out of it."

"So Gerald might have continued stealing from you if he hadn't died," Keya said, regarding Larry.

"Now I know where you're going with this," Larry protested.

"I did not tinker with his lights because he was taking money from my honesty box. I had no idea and, as I told you at the time, if I'd wanted to stop any of the lights working, I'd have altered one of the existing sets, not a new one I had no idea he'd bought."

Keya sipped her tea, considering Larry, who appeared to be telling the truth. But if Glenda had invited him into the house to hang a picture or sort out another DIY job that Gerald was too busy to help her with, he could easily have seen the new decoration lying in the study.

And if Gerald had left the control box on display? But then surely Gerald would have checked the wiring before screwing on the lid.

She popped a piece of fruitcake into her mouth.

This was all pure speculation.

"Oh, here he comes again," Glenda commented.

"Who?" asked Keya, looking out of the window into the fading light. She couldn't see anyone walking up the garden path.

But Glenda was at the other end of the table, and her view was of her front garden and Annie's, and to the road beyond them.

"Your inspector. He's been very attentive and supportive towards Annie. She might appear to have it all together, particularly when she had me to look after. But now Bart's death has finally hit her; she's close to breaking point."

"Inspector Evans lived with his mother, and she died earlier this year, so I guess he understands how you and Annie feel, losing someone so close." But the inspector hadn't mentioned coming to Limes Lane. Maybe he'd asked her to help Sujin, as he felt he was too close to the case.

Keya finished her cup of tea and said to Glenda, "Thank you, and now it's time I returned to the police station."

CHAPTER TWENTY-SEVEN

K eya went in search of Sujin as soon as she arrived back at Cirencester Police Station on Tuesday afternoon.

The noise of drunken shouting and singing became louder as she approached the custody area.

She didn't envy the officers working there during the festive period. She'd spent several years dealing with drunk and disorderly complaints and had always tried her best not to arrest people who couldn't help themselves.

But sometimes, when they became violent or she feared they might harm themselves, others, or property, she had no choice but to take action.

Sujin was playing Christmas carols, which she knew blocked out most of the noise from the custody area and helped him concentrate.

Entering his room, she removed the transparent evidence bag and said, "I think I found the source of the feathers."

Sujin took the bag and held it up to the light, examining the contents. "Great, I'll analyse these, but they do look like a match. Where did you find them?"

"Annie Beckett's coat has a rip in it, with the insulation poking out. I managed to grab those without her noticing."

"I thought the down might be from a pillow, but a jacket makes more sense. Thanks for getting them," Sujin said gratefully.

"Does this make Annie Beckett our prime suspect?" Keya asked him.

"It certainly places her at the scene. But by the sounds of it, she often visited Glenda, so it's not conclusive. Do you think she'd know how to alter the lights?"

"I was wondering about that. If I saw an open box with some electric wires on a table, and I was fed up with Gerald's bright lights, then I might decide to change the wires around so the decoration didn't work. But not knowing anything about electrics, I might do it without realising the possible consequences."

"Like electrocuting Gerald when he plugged it in."

"Precisely," Keya agreed.

"So your thinking is that someone who didn't know about electrics altered the wiring, not with the intention of hurting Gerald, but just to make sure the illuminated elf didn't work. But wouldn't there have been an easier way to do that? Like damaging the lights themselves, or…" Sujin's voice trailed off.

"I guess if the person damaged the elf, Gerald could claim it was faulty and ask for a replacement. But he couldn't do that with the control box because he shouldn't have converted it from battery to mains power."

"Of course, I'd forgotten that," Sujin admitted. He looked up at Keya, rubbing his neck with his free hand.

"What is it?" she asked, noticing his anxious expression.

"Have you seen any of your teammates since you arrived back?"

"No, I came straight to see you."

"Then I think you should. Ryan's hot under the collar about something."

Keya left Sujin's workroom, wondering what was bothering Ryan. She strode into the team room, and Ryan looked up from his desk, breathing out in relief. "I need to show you something."

He picked up his phone, tapped it, and handed it to Keya. She watched a video play, realising it was one of her and Ryan outside

Glenda's house after Bart's death, when she'd told the onlookers to stop bothering grieving relatives.

"I suppose that's trending as an example of how the police suppress individuals' rights to do as they please," Keya remarked.

She was annoyed that in a situation like this, where she was trying to protect the widow of a dead man, her actions and words were taken out of context, making her look insensitive and authoritarian.

"Something like that, yes," Ryan agreed, his ears turning red. "But there is a small countermovement of people supporting you for standing up for the grieving family."

"Whichever way people choose to look at it, I'm sure the inspector won't be happy, as we don't need this type of publicity just before the chief constable announces his plans for our team. By the way, do you know where he is?" she asked, fishing for an answer.

"No, he said he had something personal to take care of. Which isn't like him. And he's been shut away in his office with the door closed ever since you left."

Keya wondered if that had anything to do with Annie Beckett.

She glanced down at the phone, which was now playing another video. This one had been taken on the evening of Gerald's death as the inspector was arriving at the scene. There he was, meeting Larry, Glenda, and Annie on the garden path as Larry gathered up his basket of teacups.

And then the inspector uncharacteristically took Annie's hand and… Keya stopped the video, clicked the rewind symbol, and stared at the screen as the video played the scene again.

She watched as the inspector took Annie's hand and brushed against the rip in her coat.

"Can I borrow this to show Sujin?" Keya asked, and without waiting for a reply, she hurried from the room.

Back in the custody suite, she pushed open Sujin's door without knocking. "Look at this!" she exclaimed.

Blinking, Sujin took Ryan's phone and watched the video. "What am I looking at?" he asked.

"The point where the inspector shakes hands with Annie Beckett."

"He seems quite captivated by her. Is that what you mean?"

"Does he?" Keya took the phone back and pressed rewind. This time, she watched the inspector's face as he met Annie. Sujin was right. He was certainly attracted to her.

"No." Keya hit rewind again. "Look at his hand brushing against Annie's sleeve," she instructed as she handed the phone back. "At the point where Annie has a rip in her jacket."

Sujin studied the video several more times.

"So it's quite possible," Sujin concluded as he handed the phone back to Keya, "that Annie was nowhere near the exterior plug and the small feather got snagged on it during the inspector's examination."

"Yes. That's called a transfer of evidence, isn't it?"

Sujin looked up, smiling proudly. "Yes, it is. We'll make a crime scene manager of you yet."

Keya narrowed her eyes. "That was one of the courses Ryan told me about."

"I know. He said I should speak to you about applying as the applications have to be submitted by the end of this week."

"They do? But I have to work at the café tomorrow, and the inspector wants this case—well, both cases—resolved by the end of the week."

Sujin stood up, placed his hands on Keya's shoulders, and said, "All of which can manage without you while you concentrate on your application. That is, if you want to apply for the course."

"Should I?" she asked, staring into his eyes. They were soft and kind.

"I think so." Sujin let go of her. "But then I am biased. I work with crime scene managers, and I love forensics."

"But won't it be too technical for me?"

"You will have to learn the procedures for collecting evidence in detail, but you know a lot about that from a practical point of view already. And what those with a science background lack is the experience to rank the evidence. Hundreds, if not thousands, of pieces can be collected from a major crime scene, and it would be your job to select the most important ones to send to the lab for testing. And you also know that where a body is found is not necessarily the crime scene. That could be elsewhere."

"Like Gerald's case, where the lights were probably tampered with in his study cum workroom. But it's pretty clear that Bartholomew died at the scene when he fell off the ladder. Do you have the results of his post-mortem yet?"

"Sorry, I'm still waiting. There was a pile-up on the M5 today, and several people were killed, so that'll have priority. But returning to the course, do you want to apply?"

"I need to think about it," Keya said, and she left to give Ryan's phone back and finally write up her reports.

CHAPTER TWENTY-EIGHT

K eya arrived at the café at half-past eight on Wednesday morning. The day was grey, and the heavy, dark clouds threatened rain.

She smiled at the Christmas tree Gilly had placed beside the antique centre's large oak front door. Had she been influenced by the café's "natural decoration" theme?

Probably, Keya thought, as the tree was adorned with strands of wooden beads and rustic ornaments. Round slices of dried orange, tied with red ribbon, gave off a fruity scent, and a large wooden heart topped the tree.

Subtle fairy lights, presumably battery-operated, twinkled softly. It was a simple, attractive, and unassuming invitation to enter the antique centre.

Inside, Keya heard the low murmur of voices as she walked past rows of slumbering stalls and entered the unlocked café. Smiling, she inhaled the comforting aroma of gingerbread mixed with Christmas spices and brandy. Weaving between empty tables and chairs, she found Mick baking in the kitchen.

"How long have you been here?" she asked.

"About an hour. I soaked some dried fruit last night so I could make a batch of Christmas cakes this morning before we need to use the oven. We got five orders yesterday."

"That's good, but don't overwhelm yourself cooking for those and for the café."

"I don't mind the baking side, but I'll leave the decorating to you and Monica."

Fair enough, Keya thought. The cakes would need decorating. She'd discuss it with Monica later.

Keya made herself a cup of tea using the kitchen kettle. While the café was still quiet, she sat down at a table and opened her laptop.

She hadn't slept well and had woken from a strange dream where she was conducting a crime scene search at Glenda's house, but they couldn't find any evidence because the inflatable decorations kept moving around.

The dream made her think more seriously that morning about applying for a spot on the crime scene manager course. If the police were willing to pay for her to take it, why not give it a shot?

She continued reading about the work she could do with the qualification. It was specialised, and there were only a few trained officers in each geographical area. They covered major crimes spanning several police forces.

She liked the idea of working on big cases. And advising senior officers.

Smiling to herself, Keya realised she loved that idea. No more being talked down to or dismissed. Not that Inspector Evans did that, and Chief Inspector Greg had always been respectful, but many officers still looked down on her. It was one reason she wasn't keen on joining a large team at headquarters in Gloucester.

As a crime scene manager, she'd lead the team of investigators and specialists, ensure the evidence potential of a crime scene was maximised, and oversee the effective processing of it.

Wow. That was quite a responsibility. But Sujin was right. It was something she was already doing, just on a smaller scale.

Her enthusiasm dimmed slightly when she read that she'd need to ensure crime scenes were processed according to protocol. She understood why, though, as it ensured the safety of everyone on the scene and maintained the chain of evidence.

She also agreed with the need for effective communication between everyone involved. She'd be good at that, she thought, coordinating the expertise of forensic specialists with the often single-minded approach of some officers.

Still, the role would be challenging. And so would the course. Even with her experience, she knew there'd be a lot to learn, particularly about forensics, pathology, and crime scene analysis. Was it something she really wanted to take on?

She still had the café to run. Wasn't that enough?

Rubbing her chin, Keya looked up as Zivah entered the café and waved. Keya watched her younger sister. She'd maintained her slim figure, despite having Kaami. She also had a loving, respectful husband and a beautiful baby.

Zivah reached Keya's table and declared, "I'm so pleased you asked me to come in this morning. Sorry I can't cover this afternoon, but I can't miss the nursery play. Kaami is a sheep, and I found the perfect onesie for him. Amma's so excited to watch it with me."

Zivah's enthusiasm was infectious, and Keya couldn't help but smile.

"But you looked serious when I came in. Everything okay?" Zivah asked.

"I was just thinking about the likelihood of our team being disbanded, and what my options are if it is," Keya admitted.

"Aren't you going to take the redundancy money and focus on the café?" Zivah asked.

Keya leaned back, looking up at her sister. "I thought that's what I wanted, but then Ryan and Sujin suggested I apply for a crime scene manager course."

"What would that lead to?"

"Well, I wouldn't have to give up police work completely. Instead of being based at a single station, I'd be more independent, working with several police authorities and assisting groups like the British Transport Police. I'd still get to choose which cases to take, but I'd be working on some major crimes."

"And you'd like that?"

"Yes. Is it wrong to want to run a café and catch criminals?"

"Not at all," Zivah said affectionately. "It sounds like a perfect balance. Just like I love being a mum, but I'm also grateful to you for giving me the chance to work in the café when I need a break."

"You don't mind coming in?"

"Not at all! I miss the bustle and meeting people. Don't tell Amma, though. You know how she feels about me putting Kaami in nursery. But I'm thinking of increasing his hours so I can work more shifts here."

"I'd love for you to work more, but Amma will definitely blame me for your 'dereliction of parental duties,'" Keya said with a grin.

"Too true, big sis. But I'd better get to work. Here come our first customers."

Keya closed her laptop. She needed to help set up the café for the day and serve customers. But at least she'd made a decision. She was going to apply for the course.

There's no harm in applying, she thought. In fact, she really hoped she'd be accepted.

Partway through the morning, Keya's shoulder really began to ache.

Zivah saw her clutching it and asked, "Is it sore?"

"Yes. I fell over one of Gerald's Christmas decorations on Monday."

"And what did your doctor say?"

"I don't know," Keya replied evasively. "I haven't contacted him."

Zivah stared at her, her lips drawn together in an excellent impersonation of their mother.

"OK, OK. I'll make an appointment," Keya agreed.

"Now," Zivah insisted.

Keya collected empty hot chocolate cups from a table and carried them through to the kitchen.

"Dust the worktop with icing sugar so the marzipan doesn't stick," Monica was instructing Maitri.

Maitri turned round and said to Keya in an excited but nervous voice, "Monica is showing me how to decorate Christmas cakes. We're doing some with a layer of marzipan covered in fondant icing and white icing star decorations. And others will be plainer with pretty patterns created from nuts, cherries, and dried fruit."

"Well done, sis. And I hear we're getting quite a few orders."

"Yes, and I'm sure there'll be more after we've decorated and displayed these ones."

"Don't overstretch the kitchen," Keya warned. "The cakes take time to bake, and I don't want Mick working through the night."

Mick, who was stirring something in a plastic mixing bowl, turned and said, "Would you consider giving me a bonus if I did? An ad came through this morning for low-cost holidays to Morocco in January, and it looks like a fascinating place."

Keya, knowing how hard Mick worked and his wish to travel and see the world, replied, "It's certainly something we could consider."

Mick grinned and returned to his mixing bowl.

Monica removed a block of creamy-coloured marzipan from its packet and placed it on the worktop.

Keya left the kitchen, but as she passed her middle sister, Zivah mouthed, "Doctor."

Stopping beside Norman's drinks counter, Keya dialled the number for her specialist at Cirencester Hospital.

"Sergeant Varma," the doctor's PA greeted her. "We wondered when we'd be hearing from you. Dr Kosberg can't remember signing you back on for duty, yet we've seen videos of you at Limes Lane where those two men died."

"Oh, I see. Well, I'm living there at the moment, not where the men died, but with my sister further along the street, and I happened to be there when Gerald Sadler died."

"I heard he went with quite a bang," giggled the receptionist.

Ignoring the pun and deciding she better not divulge any more, Keya said, "I fell over earlier this week and my shoulder aches. I thought it would have started to feel better by now, but it hasn't."

"Let me see," said the receptionist in her professional tone. "Can you make tomorrow morning at half past ten?"

"Tomorrow, Thursday. Any chance you could make it earlier?" Keya asked.

"I could squeeze you in at eight thirty, before Dr Kosberg's morning surgery?"

"If you could. That would be great."

"Tomorrow at eight thirty then."

CHAPTER TWENTY-NINE

Without Millie or Zivah working as front of house at the café on Wednesday afternoon, Keya was kept busy greeting and seating customers and taking their orders. As she could only carry light trays of food and drinks, she recruited Maitri to help serve.

"This is great," Maitri said. "I enjoy the work I'm doing in the kitchen, but I prefer speaking to customers. And loads of them are interested in our Christmas baking orders and hamper gifts."

"Don't exhaust yourself, or Monica and Mick," Keya warned her again.

Finally, at a quarter to four, Keya was able to sit down with a cup of Darjeeling tea and her laptop. She opened the online application form for the crime scene manager course.

Her phone pinged, and when she opened it, she smiled at the photos Zivah had sent of Kaami in his sheep onesie at the nursery school play. He looked so sweet. Her mother would be very proud of him.

Back to the form. The first section was easy enough to fill out with her date of birth, and when she joined the police force and the roles she'd had to date.

The second section was trickier as it asked for relevant experience.

Did that mean the crimes she'd worked on or the forensic experience she'd had?

She called Sujin.

"Hi, are you calling about that feather?" Sujin asked when, after several rings, he answered his phone.

"Er, no. Why?"

"Then you haven't heard the news?"

"I've been working at the café all day."

"Inspector Evans resigned."

"He what?" Keya exclaimed.

Several customers turned towards her with concerned expressions. She smiled apologetically back at them and then said to Sujin, "Why?"

"I'm not sure exactly, but I hope I didn't prompt it. I told him about the feather, which I discovered on Gerald's external plug, and that we'd traced it to the down filling in Annie's jacket. He immediately became defensive and protested that Annie had nothing to do with Gerald's death. With either death. He became rather red and agitated. He definitely has a soft spot for Annie."

"Which is not helpful in the middle of an investigation. What did he say when you suggested he was the cause of the transfer?" Keya enquired.

"It stopped his blustering. He was silent and then admitted that his behaviour at the crime scene was unprofessional, even negligent, and threatened to derail the investigation. He apologised, which is a first, and excused himself."

"We all make mistakes, but his reaction seems a bit extreme."

"I thought so too," Sujin agreed.

"But I went back to my workroom to continue checking the fingerprints I took from Gerald's ladder, and it was only when I ventured out to the kitchen for some water that Stan told me about the inspector's resignation. I think he must have gone straight to see Chief Inspector Greg after he finished talking to me."

"But why this case? And why now?" Keya wondered aloud. "Do you think it was prompted by the review team and he's jumping rather than being pushed?"

"I asked Stan the same question, but he said the inspector thought he'd be shunted to some soulless position to work out the rest of his time."

"Which he'd hate," concluded Keya.

"I agree. And then Stan said something strange."

"Oh yes? What?"

"He was murmuring to himself, but he said something about the inspector getting the job down under. Do you know what that means?"

"I've no idea. Is it a company?"

"The only down under I know is a song title or, of course, a reference to Australia."

"Can you imagine the inspector and his brown suits in the Australian outback?"

Both Keya and Sujin laughed, which broke the thread of their conversation.

"Hopefully, I'll find out more tomorrow when I come into the station," Keya said. "After my doctor's appointment."

"Nothing serious, I hope?" Sujin queried.

"So do I. But my shoulder still aches after my fall in Gerald's garden and Zivah, quite rightly, insisted I had it checked out."

There was a pause before Sujin suggested, "I thought we might do something tonight or tomorrow?"

Keya remembered the reason she'd called.

"Actually ..."

"Yes?" Sujin replied in an amused tone.

"Can you help me fill out my application form for the crime scene manager course?"

"You're applying? That's brilliant! Come over tonight, around seven. I'll cook, as you've been busy in the café all day, and we'll work through it."

"Thanks. I'll see you later."

As soon as Keya finished her call, Maitri appeared by her side and asked, "What was that all about? Who were you shouting at?"

"I didn't make too much noise, did I?" Keya said in a worried tone. "I was just so shocked to hear that Inspector Evans has resigned."

"Is that such a surprise? You said your department is likely to be split up, and I can't imagine him working for some by-the-book, uni-educated young overachiever. Or advising a group of pensioners on how to protect themselves and their homes. He's old. Isn't he retiring soon, anyway?"

"I think he has a couple more years to do, but Stan said something about him getting another job."

"Like Ryan?"

"Yes, it's sad to think of my team breaking up."

"True, but it also gives you new opportunities. Zivah said you might apply for a course, like me. In fact, can we discuss it sometime?"

"Sure, let me finish and submit my application, and then we can sit down together."

"Fab."

That evening, Keya arrived at Sujin's house in Highworth just before seven. She sniffed at the delicious nutty and soy aroma.

"I hope that tastes as good as it smells," she said as she stepped into the open doorway of the small kitchen.

"Vegetarian ramen noodles. I adapted my mum's recipe. I hope you like it?"

"I'm sure I will," Keya replied, her mouth already watering.

Keya set the table in the corner of the living room while Sujin dished out their supper. He carried through two bowls of noodles in a creamy sauce, with a selection of vegetables and pieces of dried seaweed sprinkled over the top.

"Delicious," Keya said after taking her first mouthful. "My family would love this."

"Maybe I could cook it for them. Say on Christmas Eve when you're all busy preparing for the next day?"

"I'll certainly suggest it to Zivah, but our Christmas celebrations will be tame compared with what you're used to. Zivah and Kaami have been invited to the family service on Christmas morning at the church on Limes Lane and I thought I might go with them. Do you want to come, or would you rather keep Aadi company?"

"I'd like to come with you. My father's family are devout churchgoers, and it is Christmas."

"That will be nice. A proper family service."

"It will be," agreed Sujin, taking Keya's hand. "And I've been thinking more about that."

Keya felt her hand tense in Sujin's.

"I know you're happy here, and I'm delighted you're applying to go on the crime scene manager course ..."

"Is this about the position you've been offered in Glasgow? The supervisor one?" Keya interjected, her voice rising.

"In part, yes. I told the chief constable's admin team that I'd been offered the position in Scotland and that I was considering taking it."

Keya twirled her fork, wrapping noodles around it as she asked, "And how did they respond?"

"They contacted me today and asked if I'd be interested in a cross-division role, working on high-profile cases and coordinating the forensic teams." Sujin grinned. "It sounds like my ideal job. Plus, it means staying here rather than moving back to Glasgow. I'll also need to take the crime scene manager course."

Keya groaned. "Does that mean I'll lose my place to you?"

Though she was relieved to hear he wouldn't be moving.

"I don't think so. I said I knew about the course as an excellent police colleague at Cirencester was applying for it and I'd find it really helpful to have her – you – on the course to explain the police jargon and investigative side of major crime cases."

"Did they go for it?"

"I hope so. Won't it be fun learning together?" Sujin grinned enthusiastically, but Keya felt inadequate.

She looked down at the tasty bowl of food Sujin had prepared.

"Don't you want us to study together?" Sujin asked, sounding both anxious and perplexed.

"It's not that," Keya admitted, looking up and making eye contact with him. "What if everyone on the course has a forensics background like you? How will I keep up?"

"They won't. It's a mix of police officers, crime scene investigators, and forensic specialists. That way, everyone has something to contribute. And you more than most, as you've been involved in such a range of cases. I've already learnt loads from you!"

"You have?" she smiled bashfully.

"Of course I have. You're an excellent investigative officer. And a wonderful and considerate girlfriend. Now eat up, and then we can complete and submit your application form."

CHAPTER THIRTY

K eya arrived at Cirencester Hospital in time for her half-past eight appointment with Dr. Kosberg.

The hospital smelled clean and fresh, and the section she was in was modern, reminding her more of a school or nursing home than a functioning hospital.

She liked the curved edges of the department desks and the use of pinks and purples to accent certain walls, breaking up the creamy-grey colour scheme.

"Sergeant Varma, you're looking well!" Dr. Kosberg greeted her cheerfully. He had short, slightly curly light-brown hair, a ready smile and a positive demeanour.

"But I hear you haven't been taking my advice and resting. And you're involved in another investigation."

"It's my arm which is troubling me, not my brain," Keya protested. "Besides, I couldn't stand by when someone died in front of me."

"I understand, and what seems to be the trouble?"

"I tripped over an inflatable Christmas decoration and my left shoulder has ached since the fall."

"That's the reason you were put on sick leave. Not because you aren't capable of doing your job, but because your body is not up to handling unforeseen incidents. Now jump up onto the bed and sit facing me."

Keya did as instructed and removed her jacket and shirt so the doctor could move her arm one way and then the other and prod her shoulder.

"No swelling, and the mobility is excellent. Before the fall, were you feeling more confident using your arm?"

"I guess I was. In fact, I think I sometimes forgot I had a problem with it."

"That's certainly encouraging. Normally, I would ask you to come back in a week or two for another checkup before signing you back on for work. But as it's nearly Christmas, perhaps we should wait until the New Year."

Dr. Kosberg turned away, but Keya said, "Actually, it would really help if you could sign me back on before Christmas. I've applied for a course, and I may not get a place if I'm on indefinite sick leave."

The doctor paused before turning to face Keya. He tugged at his chin. "I can't sign you fit for duty yet, but I can certainly update and submit my notes and say that in my opinion, with another three weeks of recuperation, you should be fit and able to start work at the beginning of January."

"Thank you," Keya said, hoping that would be enough for her to obtain a place on the crime scene manager course.

Keya's next stop was Cirencester Police Station.

Other officers ceased their conversations when she approached and began again after she'd passed. Ducking into her team room, she was grateful to see Ryan already at his desk and she couldn't help glancing at the inspector's open door.

"You've heard the news?" Ryan stated in a flat tone.

"Sujin told me," replied Keya.

"I thought you might need this," Stan said, and she turned to face him as he offered her a mug of tea.

Stan continued, "And it might be easier for you both if you found something to do away from the station today."

"You're probably right, but we should go over the cases first and …" Keya glanced at the inspector's door as her voice trailed off.

Sujin stepped into the team room and, eyeing Keya's left arm, he asked, "Everything all right?"

"Yes. In fact, the doctor was pleased with my progress and said I should be able to return to work in the New Year. Whatever that looks like." She smiled ruefully.

Warren and another young officer laughed as they stumbled through the door. Warren caught himself when he saw the others staring at him. His friend nudged him and laughed before leaving the room.

"Close the door, can you, Warren?" Keya instructed, taking charge.

The irony wasn't lost on her that she'd just been told she couldn't be signed back for work until January and here she was, taking charge of two cases. But needs must in a small team.

Perhaps the review team was right to recommend their team be wound up and for major crimes to be dealt with by a team at headquarters which had several inspectors who could cover for each other.

Warren sloped across to sit behind his desk.

Sujin perched on the desk next to Ryan's, and Stan leaned against the end wall.

Keya began, "Despite what's happening, we still have two open cases which the inspector," she paused, "which we need to resolve as soon as possible. Sujin, let's start with you. Has the post-mortem been carried out on Bartholomew's body yet?"

"No, but they promised they'd try to fit it in today."

"Good. Is there any other forensic evidence we should be following up?" Keya asked.

"Um," Sujin began uncertainly. "I know this is a sore point, but despite the inspector insisting he transferred the down feather from Annie Beckett's coat to the external plug which Gerald used, and he probably did …"

"We need to follow it up and speak to both parties?" suggested Keya.

"Yes."

"Anything else?" Keya asked, buying herself time while she considered how to tackle the inspector and what was clearly a sensitive subject.

"I've finished processing the fingerprints I took from the ladder. There are a number of them. I've isolated Gerald's and Bartholomew's, but I couldn't identify several other sets as they're not in our system."

"And you'd like us to find out whose they are?" Keya suggested.

"Yes, even if it's just for the paperwork, but I'd be interested in knowing who touched the ladder."

"His wife?" Warren suggested.

"Both wives are who I'd start with, and then, if you can, collect all the neighbours' prints, including Larry's."

Keya leaned back against her desk. She paused before saying, "Thank you for the update, and can you let me know as soon as the post-mortem has been carried out?"

She looked at Stan and asked, "Do you fancy the rest of the morning out of the station?"

Stan grinned. "I wouldn't say no to that offer."

"Good, because I want you to join me in interviewing Inspector Evans."

Stan's smile faltered.

"You heard Sujin. We need to follow up the appearance of the feather, even though the inspector admitted transferring it and took the drastic action of resigning. We also have to consider the scenario where he didn't make the transfer, and the feather was already on the plug."

"He won't like it if you try to implicate Annie Beckett," warned Stan.

"I'm not implicating anyone at this point, just following the evidence. There could be several explanations, such as Bartholomew borrowing his wife's jacket."

Ryan snorted.

"OK, his arm would barely have fitted into it, but you know where

I'm coming from. There might be different angles than just the obvious ones."

In the pause that followed, Warren said, "I don't understand what mistake was so serious that it made the inspector resign? I like working in this team, but with you on sick leave, Sarge, the inspector leaving, and Ryan trying to find a new job … well, there'll be nothing left of it."

Stan gave him a sympathetic look and said, "I doubt there will be anyway after the chief constable makes his announcement. But if you play your cards right, you might be offered a position on the county murder squad."

"I'm not sure I want to work in the headquarters," Warren complained.

"Let's stop speculating, shall we, and concentrate on the cases at hand," Keya said, hoping she sounded authoritative. "Stan and I will visit the inspector while you, Ryan, take Warren to gather fingerprints from Larry, Glenda, Annie, Gabrielle, and Jackson. Let's maintain a professional outlook on these cases and resolve them for the inspector as soon as we can."

CHAPTER THIRTY-ONE

K eya drove her own car to the small Cotswold town of Tetbury, close to King Charles and Queen Camilla's private country residence, Highgrove House.

Inspector Evans' Cotswold stone, double-fronted terraced house, which fronted London Road, one of the main routes leading into the town, was a more modest affair. For as long as Keya had known him, he'd lived there with his mother, and the furnishings reflected this.

The kitchen would now be considered retro with its Formica cupboards, and she remembered the faded yellow woodchip wallpaper in the dining room where Mrs. Evans' hospital bed had been located, and the floral wallpaper and matching old-style three-piece suite in the living room.

Finding a kerbside parking space a little distance from the inspector's house, Keya and Stan walked along the pavement as the front door opened and the inspector stepped out and stared at them.

Keya glanced at Stan, but he refused to look at her, and she guessed he'd warned the inspector that they were coming. Old loyalties ran deep, but there was nothing she could do about it now.

"Come in," invited Inspector Evans. "I have tea and biscuits ready. No cake these days since mother passed away, as they're not good for my waistline."

Keya noticed that the inspector wasn't wearing his usual brown suit trousers. Instead, he had on a new-looking pair of fawn cotton trousers.

The change in clothing made it seem as though he had lost some weight. The light blue, short-sleeved, collared shirt he wore no longer strained across his broad chest. She thought he looked well, with a recent haircut, though his outfit seemed a little inappropriate for the chilly winter weather.

The living room had the same floral wallpaper and faded green carpet Keya remembered, but there was no sign of the matching sofa and chairs. Instead, there was a dark-brown leather chair facing the large modern television screen.

Two retro-style dining chairs were arranged on the opposite side of a small wooden side table, which held three grey cups and a plate of biscuits.

"Please take a seat," said the inspector, indicating to the dining chairs. "I'm sorry I can't offer you something more comfortable." He didn't add why the living room was so sparsely furnished, but perhaps he wasn't used to hosting guests and hadn't felt the need to replace the old three-piece suite.

"And let me offer my apologies," the inspector began, looking at Keya. "I haven't been entirely straight with you."

Keya picked up a cup of milky tea and sipped it, while Stan crunched a chocolate Bourbon biscuit.

"I've known for a while that the chief constable has had his eye on Cirencester Police Station, and on our small team in particular. I thought when that wide-boy, Inspector Smiles ..."

Keya recalled Inspector Evans' temporary replacement, who had baffled her with investigative procedures, and remembered everyone else's nickname for him.

"He took over from me and advised that the team be wound up. But he praised us – you – for the work you did in solving Ronnie Marsh's case. When Chief Inspector Greg announced that the review team would spend time at the station, I knew we would be one of their focal points, and that I would end up spending my time until retirement doing nothing more interesting than working through mounds of paperwork."

The inspector paused and glanced at Keya. She waited patiently for him to continue.

He did. "But there aren't many opportunities for an ageing, old-style policeman in the UK's modern law enforcement. And the thought of taking early retirement and sitting around here all day…" The inspector glanced around the room with a mixture of sadness and affection. "I'd soon follow my mother into the ground."

Keya thought the inspector was being a little dramatic, but she also knew how important his job was in giving him a sense of purpose and belonging.

The inspector continued, "So Stan and I were discussing my options when he told me about an advert he'd seen for an experienced British police officer to relocate to southern Australia."

Keya's mouth fell open in surprise, and worried she'd spill her tea, she placed her mug back on the small table.

"Australia?" she repeated in a strangled voice. "You?"

"Yes, Sergeant. Me. It might appear that I haven't left the Cotswolds for twenty years, and I rarely did because of mother, but I do have an adventurous side. And after chatting to Mick in your café, he reminded me that there is so much more out there."

"But Australia? Isn't that a bit drastic?"

"No one closer to home wants my services, but the job listed qualities I have: honesty, reliability, courage, and the ability to work as a confident and decisive problem-solver. I'm good at thinking on my feet. Maybe I'm less patient, resilient, and respectful," the inspector admitted, "but I fit the rest."

He paused and gave Keya and Stan a wry smile.

"The work might not be the most exciting or challenging, but the promise of a Mediterranean climate, a friendly, laid-back lifestyle, a lower cost of living, and Australia's best beach along with some of the country's finest wine had me hooked. And of course, the fact they speak English, more or less, sealed the deal."

"So, you're taking the job?" Keya's voice was still strained, the conversation feeling somewhat surreal.

"It's mine. I've already completed the paperwork and had the online interviews, which certainly made the process simpler."

"But what about your friends?" Keya raised.

"Besides you and Stan, who do I really have? I've spent my entire life working or with my mother. And you both have families and loved ones. Who's really going to miss me?"

"We all will," Keya declared emphatically, grateful that he counted her as a friend. She might joke about the inspector and find him grumpy, even objectionable at times, but she couldn't imagine him leaving. And to the other side of the world?

"Won't you be lonely?" she reasoned.

The inspector shifted his weight in his chair and looked away.

Stan joked, "With all those sheep? It'll be like being back in Wales, just without the rain."

"So when do you start?" Keya asked, wondering how long it would take her to wrap up her life for such a major move.

"In the New Year, although as there's nothing keeping me now, I might travel early and search for somewhere to live. A place with a porch so I can sit out on an evening with a cold beer and listen to the sound of the insects or watch a game of rugby."

"That soon?" Keya exclaimed, her eyes bulging. "But what about …." Her voice trailed off. What was preventing the inspector from upping and leaving? Just this house. She looked around and took in the darker patches on the wallpaper from where pictures had been taken down. Finally, she realised that the inspector was ready to move on.

She looked at him and nodded. Why not try it out? He could always come back.

"It's a bold move," Keya admitted, "and I don't envy you starting afresh in a new place, but there will be no ties, no misconceptions, and no baggage. In fact, you can reinvent yourself in any way you wish."

The inspector smiled. A mischievous one?

Then he said, "I knew you'd understand. And why not come and visit? Stan and his wife are already planning a trip."

Stan's face reddened, and he admitted, "We've always wanted to visit Australia, but with the long flight, and, well, it's so big."

"But now they can use my place as a base. So you see, I won't be lonely after all. But thank you for your concern." He regarded her before he said, "I know you're really here to discuss the transfer of evidence at Gerald Sadler's crime scene."

"Yes, sir," Keya replied as she struggled to concentrate on the cases which still needed concluding, rather than dreaming about wide, sandy beaches. But if she was to visit anywhere, she'd be drawn to India.

"Sergeant?" queried the inspector.

"Sorry, sir." She took a deep breath, forcing herself to focus. "As you know, a small feather, known as down, was found trapped in the external plug Gerald Sadler used to connect his faulty elf light. Although someone tampered with the lights rather than the plug, it is a piece of evidence Sujin suggests we clear up before concluding the case, and …"

"It was me," interrupted the inspector. "I've seen the video, and it's clear the feather attached itself to me when I greeted Annie, and I transferred it to the plug. Annie had no reason to be anywhere near it."

"I agree that is an obvious solution, but we do have to consider Annie as a suspect and …"

"She had nothing to do with this."

Even Stan stiffened in surprise at the inspector's heated denial.

Calmly, Keya replied, "I'm sure she didn't, but you know we still have to pursue it as a line of enquiry."

"No. You don't. I'll swear that I was the one who placed the feather on the plug. Case closed."

Keya glanced at Stan, who gave her an imperceptible shake of the head.

He was right. There was no point in pursuing the matter further with the inspector. He clearly wasn't entertaining Annie's involvement in any capacity, even though he knew Keya was obliged to investigate every angle of the case.

Keya and Stan took their leave of Inspector Evans. Halfway back to her car, Keya stopped and turned round.

The inspector gave her a wave, and she waved back. She couldn't help wondering if it was the final time she'd see him.

CHAPTER THIRTY-TWO

K eya was driving herself and Stan back from Tetbury when she received a call from Ryan.

"We've collected fingerprints from Glenda and Jackson. Larry wasn't very happy about it until I told him we needed to rule him out of any wrongdoing. Gabrielle was out meeting a production company, and there's no answer from Annie's house. What do you want us to do?"

"Stan and I are heading to the station, so we'll meet you there. One of us can pop back to Limes Lane later to get Annie's and Gabrielle's prints."

They all arrived back at the station at the same time. Stan offered to make tea while Keya visited Sujin in his workroom. "Rockin' Around the Christmas Tree" could be heard through Sujin's closed door.

She knocked and waited while the music was turned down and Sujin called, "Come in."

"Hiya, we're all back. Shall we have another catch-up meeting before lunch? And then do you fancy a bite to eat somewhere?" asked Keya.

"I'd love a bowl of thick, warming soup," Sujin acknowledged. "And yes, I do need to update you all."

Keya and Sujin walked into the team room as Stan said, "And all the pictures had been removed from the walls and ..." He turned round and stopped when he saw Keya.

"You noticed that too?" Keya said. "As if the inspector has been preparing to move."

"Move where?" Sujin asked behind her.

Keya crossed to stand in front of her desk and said, "Australia. South Australia. You tell them about it, Stan," and he did.

When Stan had finished, Ryan said, "I hope he'll be OK there. South Australia is one of the larger states, the least populated, and the most arid."

"So not many sheep," Stan said.

"Er, there probably are," Ryan replied, clearly confused as to why that was relevant. "There are some amazing beaches and clear seas, if you don't mind the odd shark ..."

Keya shivered.

"And fascinating trips into the interior. Millie and I looked at going, but it's too expensive on our current wages."

Keya gulped guiltily, but it wasn't her place to fund her staff's adventurous trips abroad, although it did sound fascinating. Perhaps she should consider visiting the inspector, after all. But, as she reminded herself, she had two cases to tie up.

Turning to look at Sujin, who was perched on the spare desk nearest the door, she asked, "What do you need to update us on?"

"The results of Bartholomew Beckett's post-mortem. It'll be no surprise to you that he died from blunt force trauma."

"He hit his head when he fell off the ladder," Stan translated, standing in the doorway to Inspector Evans' office, in case anyone was in any doubt about what Sujin's words meant.

"Yes, but there were two impact points. One on the right side of his head, which makes sense. If he was falling face-first, his natural instinct would have been to turn his head. That is the injury which killed him. But there was another, more concentrated trauma area on the left side, which the pathologist was unable to account for conclusively."

"Maybe he hit his head on the way down? On the ladder, or perhaps the wall of the house," Ryan suggested.

"It wasn't the ladder because we didn't find any blood, hair, or skin when we examined it."

"That's true. What about the wall?" pressed Ryan.

"He could have done," Sujin admitted grudgingly, "but then the pathologist would probably have found stone dust in the wound."

"And he didn't," Keya concluded. "So what are the possibilities?"

"From the location and position we found him in, I'm not sure. The pathologist noted a clean cut in the wound, but didn't determine what caused it."

"Do you think it's something we should look into?" Keya asked.

Sujin gave her an apologetic smile.

"That's a yes, then."

"Sorry, I keep posing more questions rather than providing you with answers."

"Don't worry, we'll get there," Keya responded with more confidence than she felt.

"We got you some fingerprints," Warren said brightly.

"Good. Thank you. That gives me something to work on. But after lunch."

Sujin looked at Keya, but Ryan said, "Excellent idea. I saw that Café Mosaic on Market Place is doing lunchtime specials. Shall we try it?"

Keya didn't feel she should upset the harmony of the team by suggesting she and Sujin eat lunch alone, so she agreed to Ryan's suggestion.

After lunch, Keya spent the afternoon typing up reports and considering as many scenarios as she could regarding the two unsolved deaths on Limes Lane.

They really weren't much further forward than they had been at the beginning of the week, and she was beginning to wonder if these were two cases she should let go of.

Was it really in the public interest for their team to spend time looking into two deaths that both appeared accidental? But then, what else did they have to do, and these could be their last cases.

Besides, she'd sworn to help all people, however she felt about them personally. An image of Bartholomew's sneering face entered her mind.

The one good thing about the afternoon was that the ache in her left shoulder had subsided. Perhaps it had only wanted her to check in with her doctor?

Sujin had shown her the relevant parts of Bartholomew's post-mortem and the unexplained wound. There was a small sharp, clean cut in it which, she agreed, was impossible to explain from what she'd seen at the scene. But, she remembered, this hadn't been much, as Bartholomew's body had been covered by the huge inflatable Santa.

She closed down her computer, borrowed Sujin's precious mobile fingerprint scanner, which she promised not to drop or break, and drove to Limes Lane, parking outside Gabrielle's house. But it was Larry's property that caught her attention.

The framework of the stall where he'd been selling items to visitors to Gerald's Christmas display was still standing. She hadn't found any real motive for anyone to kill Gerald, but the theft of Larry's takings could be one. Would Larry really tamper with the control box?

He'd know how dangerous that would be and, as he said, if he'd wanted to get his own back on Gerald, he could have vandalised the decorations in the garden.

He was unlikely to want to harm Gerald personally, just annoy him. And hadn't he taken to standing outside his property during the busiest times, like the evening Gerald died?

It was a line of inquiry she couldn't dismiss altogether, but without firm evidence, there was nothing she could prove. She didn't think Larry had anything to do with Gerald's death, but Bartholomew's?

She remembered the interviews, and something nagged at her about a statement Larry had made. Did he know more than he was telling her?

CHAPTER THIRTY-THREE

The wooden gate had been installed across the drive at Gabrielle and Jackson's property, and it looked very smart.

Keya opened the smaller garden gate and walked up the path. As she approached the front door, the security light flicked on.

It took some time, and several rings of the doorbell, for anyone to answer although she heard Chief's distant barking.

Eventually, Gabrielle, wearing no makeup and a towel wrapped around what Keya presumed was damp hair, opened the door. Again, Keya thought how young and vulnerable she looked.

"Keya, lovely to see you. Or is it?" Gabrielle asked uncertainly.

"Nothing serious. I just need to take your fingerprints to, as they say on the TV, eliminate you from our enquiries." Keya smiled apologetically at the use of the cliché, but Gabrielle beamed with delight.

"Come in," Gabrielle invited. As Keya stepped inside, she continued, "Jackson can film us as this is just what I need for my true crime show. But I must blow-dry my hair and see to my face. Let's go upstairs, and you can tell me all about the progress you're making."

"There isn't much to tell you," Keya said, climbing the white carpeted staircase behind her host. She was intrigued to see Gabrielle's bedroom, but she was both impressed and a touch disappointed when she entered. Was this the real Gabrielle without the make-up?

The room was tastefully decorated with creams and grey, and some period furniture she thought Dotty, who knew about antiques, would be impressed with. The bed was covered with a crisp white duvet and an assortment of cushions.

Chief was curled up on a plush teal-green velvet blanket at the bottom of the bed, his long ears flopped adorably over the edge, giving him a slightly comical appearance as he slept.

"Take a seat," Gabrielle said, indicating a small stylish velvet-covered sofa at the foot of the bed.

Gabrielle removed her towel, flung it on the bed, and sat down at an antique dressing table. She secured her long, damp hair with a large clip.

"My agent has some interest for my true crime programme, but we need an edge to it. A hook of some kind, like a personal story. Do you have one, Keya, which would interest the public? I could make you a star, you know. A British-Indian female detective leading a murder investigation."

"Ah, it's not actually a murder investigation, and thanks, but I have no wish to be famous. I enjoy a quiet life."

"That's not what Zivah tells me. Think about it. Running your café would add that personal element."

"Thanks, but no. And I'm not sure these cases will have enough excitement for your show. At the moment, they're rather mundane. We only have a few unexplained pieces of evidence to clear up before we conclude them."

"Like my fingerprints?"

"Like those."

"And what is it you think I've touched?" asked Gabrielle as she lifted her mascara wand to her eye.

"Gerald's ladder, which Bartholomew fell from. Someone might have been holding it when he fell."

Gabrielle swore, surprising Keya, who stared at her host's reflection in the antique mirror.

"Sorry," Gabrielle apologised, reaching for a tissue and dabbing her eye. "I wasn't aware of anyone being with Bart in the garden. I thought he climbed the ladder on his own."

"That may be true. You said you met Glenda and Annie and walked around the side of the house together to discover Bartholomew's body. Why did you go to Glenda's? How did you know they were having tea together at Annie's?"

Gabrielle took her time dabbing her eye and reapplying mascara before she answered.

"Jackson heard a cry and, after Gerald's accident, we were worried and rushed round to see what had happened. And as for knowing about Annie and Glenda, they must have told me they were having tea together. Annie was a real help to Glenda."

"Was?"

"Before Bart's death. After that, she's been the one needing support."

"I need her fingerprints, too," commented Keya.

"Why?" asked Gabrielle sharply.

"For the same reason I require yours."

"But surely you don't think she had anything to do with … anything?"

"As I said, we need to eliminate everyone from our enquiries."

For the next five minutes, Keya sat back and watched Gabrielle go through a complex process for drying her hair.

Chief stirred slightly, raising his head to watch the activity with sleepy interest before settling back into his blanket. Another reason Keya didn't want to be famous. She was more of a wash-and-go sort of girl.

Keya spent another half an hour at Gabrielle and Jackson's house, as Gabrielle insisted Jackson film her from several different angles as she provided her fingerprints.

Keya did her best not to be filmed, but in the end, she gave up dodging the camera. How likely was it that a programme would be made about two pretty mundane suburban deaths?

She left the house wishing she could drive straight to Zivah's, but first, she needed to visit Annie and take her fingerprints. Then hopefully they could conclude that strand of the investigation.

There were no lights on at Annie's house, and she had to pick her way up the garden path in the gloom. It was much harder to see since Gerald's illuminations had been dismantled, although the reindeer and their sleigh still festooned the roof.

Keya noticed that none of the curtains were drawn, and the property had an uncharacteristic feeling of neglect about it.

At the front door, she switched on the torch of her phone and noticed the limp flowers in their pots. She was about to pick up a small metal watering can when she stopped herself.

If Annie wasn't in, perhaps Sujin could lift her prints from the watering can, and Keya could save herself or Ryan a return trip. But where was Annie? Nobody had mentioned her going to stay with friends or family, although that was totally understandable in the current circumstances.

Keya pressed the doorbell, not expecting a response, and she didn't receive one. After two more rings, she pulled on a pair of latex gloves which she'd got back into the habit of always carrying with her, and picked up the watering can.

The hairs on the back of her neck bristled as she negotiated Annie's garden path, and she had the feeling she was being watched. Sure enough, when she stepped onto the pavement and looked round, she saw Larry standing in his doorway.

For a second, their eyes met before Larry turned and entered his bungalow, closing the door behind him.

It felt synonymous with the state of Gerald's and Bartholomew's cases. Doors were being closed in her face. But did that mean someone had something to hide?

CHAPTER THIRTY-FOUR

O n Friday morning, Keya woke up determined to get to the bottom of the two deaths that had occurred just down the street from Zivah's house on Limes Lane.

Although on the surface, both deaths appeared accidental, small details that Keya couldn't put her finger on just didn't add up.

As she stared at her reflection in the bathroom mirror and brushed her teeth, she decided that she needed to visit the police station and look through the case notes. But back in her bedroom, she noticed her phone flash, and when she checked her messages, she found one from Maitri.

> Are you coming in today? You promised to
> discuss my course with me.

Her youngest sister was right. She had said she'd sit down with her, but did she have the headspace to deal with it now? No, she had to get a sense of where they were with the investigations first and decide what action, if any, to take.

With a sigh, she sent a message to Millie, hoping that she'd pass it on to Maitri.

At least she had touched base with her staff, even if her message was vague. By now, she suspected Millie understood how both she and Ryan became wrapped up in cases until they were concluded.

Keya finished dressing.

In the kitchen, she found Zivah nursing a cup of tea.

"Morning, sis," said Zivah drowsily.

"Bad night?" Keya asked.

"I'm surprised Kaami didn't wake you with all his crying. It was exhausting."

"I thought he was better now you give him medicine to soothe his tummy."

"It does help his reflux, but it doesn't stop it altogether, and sometimes, like last night, he's so uncomfortable he bawls his head off. And there's nothing Aadi or I can do about it."

"And you feel guilty you can't stop the pain?"

"Something like that," muttered Zivah, before sipping her tea.

Keya switched the kettle on and reached for the muesli.

"Do you mind if I'm late into the café this morning? I'll get Kaami ready for Aadi to drop at nursery, but I think I need to go back to bed."

"Sure," Keya replied. She could hardly tell her exhausted sister that no, she was needed at the café because she was working on a case.

"You're not going to the café this morning, are you?" Zivah asked as Keya removed a container of mixed berries from the fridge together with a tub of natural yoghurt.

"I just need to pop into the station first," Keya replied, trying to sound casual.

"Don't worry. I know you need to get to the bottom of Gerald and Bart's deaths. And the whole street needs closure on them before Christmas. Let me grab a shower. I'm sure I'll feel better after that, and I can cover at the café."

Keya turned and protested, "There's no need to."

But Zivah raised her hand. "It's a Friday, and it's just over a week until Christmas. You can't afford to be short-staffed." She left the room.

Guiltily, Keya ate her breakfast, wondering if it was fair to expect her sister and the staff to pick up the slack at the café while she focused on her police work. But wasn't that why she had promoted Millie to front of house?

So she and Zivah didn't have to be there all the time. Maybe she should consider hiring someone else to join the team, especially if she was going to be away on the crime scene manager course.

And what about the apprenticeships Millie and Maitri were interested in? Would she lose two more members of staff?

But that was not a problem for today.

Rinsing her bowl, she grabbed her bag, coat, scarf, hat, and gloves, and left for Cirencester Police Station.

It was quiet when she arrived, and she checked her watch. Just after eight o'clock. Making a fresh cup of tea, she carried it through to her team room and settled at her desk to read through the case files for Gerald Sadler's and Bartholomew Beckett's deaths.

She jotted down inconsistencies and queries in her notebook and was so engrossed that she hadn't noticed Ryan arrive until Stan stepped into the room and asked, "Anyone want a brew?"

Keya glanced at her black watch. Nearly nine o'clock. She'd done well and only had the final statements from Bartholomew's neighbours to re-read.

"I'd love a fresh cup, Stan," she said, "and I'd also like to call a team meeting for quarter past nine. Can you let Warren and Sujin know?"

"Sure. Do you have a new lead?"

Keya smiled regretfully and replied, "If only."

Keya was just completing the case notes when Warren entered the team room, crossed to Ryan's desk, and asked, "Are you going to the match tomorrow?"

"A home game against Swindon Town. Definitely."

Keya knew they were talking about football. She read the final section of the case notes before sitting back. There were definitely aspects of the cases that needed clarifying.

"Here you go," Stan said, placing a mug of tea on her desk. "Sorry for the delay, but I bumped into the chief inspector. He said we're not to miss his coffee and chat at ten this morning."

Keya groaned. That was all she needed. But perhaps he'd have more news about the future of the station, so she and the team better not miss it.

Sujin appeared and sat down behind the spare desk next to Ryan. Warren sat opposite him, and Stan wheeled Inspector Evans' chair into the open doorway of his empty office.

"Thanks, everyone." Keya wasn't sure what she was thanking them for, but she ploughed on. "I want to go through the two deaths that occurred on Limes Lane. Inspector Evans was right to want them concluded and passed on to the coroner's office if not by today, then by next week. I'm sure both families will want closure before Christmas."

She looked around at her colleagues, who all nodded their agreement.

"Let's see how far we get before Chief Inspector Greg's weekly get-together. Starting with Gerald Sadler. Are we in agreement that he died as a result of the faulty controls on the illuminated elf, and that he was electrocuted when he plugged the decoration into the external socket?"

Keya looked to Sujin for confirmation.

"That's correct. And that the electrocution caused Gerald's heart to stop."

"So from all appearances an accident, except that the control box, which we know Gerald converted from battery to mains power, was incorrectly wired. Gerald's mistake, or deliberately altered by someone else?"

Nobody answered her rhetorical question.

"Did someone need knowledge of, or experience with, electrics to alter the wires on the control box?"

Again, Keya looked at Sujin.

"I can't give you a definitive answer. All I can say is it would help, and why would someone who didn't have such experience think to tamper with the controls?"

"Like pushing him off a ladder," muttered Stan, and then caught himself, probably realising what he'd just said.

"We'll come on to that," said Keya dryly. "And then there's opportunity. As Larry told us, if he'd wanted to harm Gerald, he'd have tampered with one of the many lights already in the garden, not a new one he didn't know Gerald had bought, which he couldn't access, as it was in the Sadlers' house."

"That's not right though, is it?" Ryan said. And then his cheek flushed.

"Go on," encouraged Keya.

"I don't want to incriminate Larry, but he did go inside to help Glenda put up shelves and complete other projects around the house."

"And he might have a motive," Keya stated.

"Larry?" Ryan questioned. "I didn't think he had much time for Gerald, or Bart, for that matter."

"I think Gerald was stealing from Larry's honesty box and, if Larry reached the same conclusion before me, he might have tampered with the lights intending to get his own back on Gerald."

"Larry wasn't the only one with a grudge against Gerald," Ryan protested. "What about Bart? He was always complaining about the lights lowering the tone of the street and affecting the value of his house."

"But what opportunity did he have? Or knowledge of electronics?" reasoned Keya. "If I read him right, he'd have been far less subtle. Look how he marched round to the Sadlers' after Gerald's death to remove the giant Santa on his own."

"I'm surprised he didn't smash the lights earlier, or threaten Gerald face-to-face," Stan commented.

"Do you know if he did, Ryan?" Keya asked.

Ryan shook his head. "I haven't heard of him threatening Gerald. And I tend to agree with you. I can't see him fiddling with complex wiring. He was a smash-it-up type of guy."

"Shame, it would have been tidy to blame him for Gerald's death,"

Keya mused. "That leaves the down feather, which was the cause of the inspector's swift departure."

"What motive would Annie have to harm Gerald? She had her own husband to deal with," Ryan observed.

"True," agreed Stan.

Sujin sat up and said, "Despite it initially appearing extreme for Inspector Evans to resign because of a possible transfer of evidence, having re-watched the video online, and others taken at the time, I think the feather did brush onto his hand or sleeve and then lodge itself in the plug casing when the inspector picked it up."

"So should we close that as a line of enquiry?" Keya asked.

"Unless you have any reason to suspect Annie for Gerald's death, I'd say yes," Sujin confirmed.

"If we rule Annie out for the moment, who does that leave as possible suspects?" Keya asked.

"Larry," Ryan said grudgingly.

"His wife," suggested Warren.

They all stared at him.

"What? I know you haven't mentioned her, and husbands are more likely to kill wives than the other way round, but it's still most likely that a person is murdered by someone close to them. And who else was close to Gerald?"

CHAPTER THIRTY-FIVE

K eya stared at Warren and said, "That's an excellent point. We haven't really considered Glenda in her husband's death. She seemed so vulnerable and, dare I say it, pathetic after Gerald's death, but when I popped round on Tuesday, I was struck by how confident and self-assured she was."

"You mean it was just an act after Gerald's death?" Sujin enquired.

Keya considered what she meant, then replied slowly, "No, I think she really was hit hard by it, but my initial assessment of her as a timid and rather incompetent housewife was probably wrong."

"She had a technical job in Bristol that she didn't want to give up, but was forced to when Gerald retired and insisted they move," Ryan said.

"That's right," Keya agreed. "She told me she was a laboratory technician."

"Then she might know about electrics and electronics," Sujin said.

"And she must have been fed up with Gerald and his obsession with lighting their house up like a Christmas tree, attracting all those people to gawp at them. What peace and privacy did that give her?" Stan raised.

A fellow police officer stuck his head round the door and said, "Time for the chief inspector's coffee and chat."

Warren pushed himself to his feet, but Keya said, "Before we take a break, are we agreed that we should look into both Larry and Glenda regarding Gerald's death?"

"Yes," chorused the others as they filed out of the room.

Keya followed them, her mind still lingering on Glenda's changed demeanour. It was a stark contrast to how she'd seen her just after Gerald's death.

Upstairs, in the open plan space where the weekly coffee and chat sessions were held, the chatter died down as Chief Inspector Greg strode to the far wall and turned to face his colleagues.

"Thank you for joining me this morning. If you were hoping for an update regarding the future of the station, then I'm afraid I don't have one. That is to say, I've had several meetings with the chief constable, and I feel confident that he will make his announcement next week, giving everyone time to absorb the news before Christmas."

The chief inspector continued to say how proud he was of everyone and how well they were handling the uncertainty during what was turning out to be another busy lead-up to Christmas.

After he'd finished, Keya was about to return to the team room when she heard, "Keya, may I have a word?"

The chief inspector preferred the casual approach.

"Yes, sir," said Keya, turning round to face him.

"How are you coping with your arm, the cases, and no Inspector Evans? I could bring someone in from headquarters, but would that really help?"

"I don't think so, sir. The team is working all angles on the cases, but we're still uncertain whether they are anything more than accidental deaths."

"And when do you think they will be concluded?" Chief Inspector Greg looked serious, and Keya realised this was the real reason he wanted to speak to her.

As Inspector Evans had hinted, it was important in the decisions about the station, and their team in particular, that the investigations were neatly tied up and not hanging over them when the chief constable made his announcement.

"We're conducting a review this morning, sir. After which, we'll follow up any outstanding leads and threads of evidence."

"What resources do you need?" asked the chief inspector.

"If you want a swift conclusion, can you approve overtime?" Keya enquired. It would be nice for the team members to receive a Christmas bonus.

"In this instance, yes. It's important to wrap up these cases. If there's nothing there, don't go looking for it. Not this time."

This was a clear warning, and while the chief inspector was usually supportive of them chasing even tenuous leads, it was clear that this time he was under pressure and needed a simple solution. But could she give him one?

She looked at Chief Inspector Greg and said, "Yes, sir. I understand."

Back in their team room, conscious of the chief inspector's unspoken direction, Keya said, "So we're agreed on the action we need to take regarding Gerald's death. Ryan and I will interview Larry and Glenda again, and if we're satisfied with the accounts they give, we'll conclude that his death was accidental and pass our recommendation on to the coroner's office."

That would certainly satisfy Chief Inspector Greg.

"Moving on to Bartholomew Beckett's death. We know he climbed the ladder, that he fell, and that he died from a head wound consistent with that fall."

Sujin didn't wait for her to look at him but immediately responded, "That's correct."

"But there are inconsistencies," Keya continued. "The second wound on his head. How was it caused? Was he alone when he fell, or was someone with him? If anyone was there, then the statements Annie and her neighbours gave were misleading at best, or downright lies."

"You think they were all lying?" Ryan asked, his eyes wide and questioning.

"Something is niggling at me. It's not necessarily what they said, although I'd like to reconsider their statements, but how they said it."

"I don't follow," said Stan.

"OK, let's start at the beginning. Inspector Evans arrived at the scene first. That in itself was unusual. Normally, he waits for me or you, Ryan, if you're on duty."

"Perhaps he knew you would drive yourself there and go to your sister's afterwards," suggested Ryan.

"True, and I'm not saying the inspector was involved, as he was at the station when Bartholomew died. At least, I presume he was. What can you tell us from a scientific point of view about the time of death?" Keya looked at Sujin.

"The body was still warm when I arrived, which is consistent with the witness statements that he'd been dead for about an hour. And rigor mortis hadn't set in, which I wouldn't expect to happen in the cold weather for at least three hours."

"So are you saying the time of death was an hour, or up to three hours before you arrived?" Keya pressed.

"Scientifically speaking, it isn't possible to pinpoint the time of death to less than three hours from when I arrived at twenty past six."

"So any time from twenty past three, which is a much wider window than we've been considering," Keya said.

Ryan wrinkled his nose before asking, "But why would one of them, or actually, all of them, lie about the time of Bart's death? Surely, we can accept what they said, and that he fell off the ladder and died. An accident, as we all presumed initially."

"Yes, but ..." Keya's voice trailed off.

"What else is bothering you?" asked Sujin.

"The inflatable Santa," Keya replied. "Gabrielle, who stood up and spoke for herself, Glenda, and Annie, said that the three of them walked round the side of the house and saw Bart lying on the ground."

"So?" Warren questioned, frowning. "What's wrong with that? We know he fell off the ladder onto the grass."

"But the first thing they would have seen, that I saw, was a giant

Father Christmas. Then they'd have noticed the parts of Bart which were visible beneath it."

Silence.

"Um," Ryan began. "Are you suggesting that Bart was lying on the ground, but the Santa was not on top of him?"

"Yes," Keya agreed, gasping with relief. "But I needed someone else to say it, to make sure it made sense."

Sujin spoke again, "I have the Santa in its deflated form. I didn't see the need to examine it, but I can, if you want me to?"

"I think you should," Keya directed. "But start with fingerprints or any obvious evidence, as that'll be quickest."

Warren said, "I still don't understand. Why try to hide Bart's body? And surely the inflatable Santa didn't kill him?"

Stan sucked air through his teeth. Then he said, "But it drew everyone's attention, and we've all presumed Bart climbed the ladder to take it down."

"And that Bart's death was an accident," Keya concluded. "It might be an accident. But in that case, why interfere with the crime scene?"

CHAPTER THIRTY-SIX

Another silence followed Keya's pronouncement that Annie, or her neighbours, might have placed the giant inflatable Santa on top of Bartholomew's body on purpose.

Finally, Ryan said, almost apologetically, "What if they were trying to hide the body from view? From the people who were videoing the decorations and the site of Gerald's death."

"I couldn't believe how many people were filming what was going on in the garden," Warren said.

"Of course, you were already there when I arrived," Keya said.

"Yes, the inspector instructed me to drive a squad car to the scene and keep the 'nosey parkers' at bay."

"So what time did you arrive?"

"At ten to six."

"And it was already dark. And Gerald's light display was on?"

"Yes, to both questions."

"I believe Gerald had most of the lights on a timer," said Ryan. "And they switched on at dusk."

"That's quite a wide timeframe. Do we know when exactly?"

"Warren could check social media while we're out interviewing Annie and Larry," Ryan suggested.

"Good call. Is that OK with you?" Keya asked Warren.

Warren smiled. He was probably pleased to have a task he knew how to do.

"All right," said Keya, gathering her thoughts. She was really trying to work methodically this morning.

"So Sujin, you'll examine the Santa, and Warren will check through social media posts. Next, the ladder."

"I can confirm," said Sujin, "that as well as both of the deceased, Glenda and Larry's prints were on it. That leaves one set unaccounted for."

"And you checked through the others who might have been involved?"

"Jackson and Gabrielle, yes, but I still need to isolate Annie's from the watering can you brought me."

Ryan, Warren, and Stan stared at Keya.

She explained, "Annie wasn't in when I visited last night, so I brought back the watering can I found beside those lovely pots of flowers outside her front door. As I couldn't see Bartholomew lifting his hand to water them, I deduced that Annie's prints should be on it."

Keya looked at Sujin and asked, "Can you look for Annie's prints first and then check them against the unidentified ones on the ladder?"

Sujin nodded.

"You don't think …" Ryan began.

Keya interrupted, "I'm not speculating. Just working through the evidence." She didn't want to be sidetracked discussing all the possible reasons Annie might have touched the ladder. Not yet, anyway.

She checked her notes and said, "Returning to our witness statements. Gabrielle was quick to say that Jackson turned the electricity off after they found Bartholomew's body, but Larry said it was him. He later changed his story and said that it was his suggestion to turn the power off, but he couldn't remember whether he or Jackson actually did it. That, I'm certain, is a lie. Larry knew exactly who went into Glenda's house and turned the power off at the fuse box. And I'm sure if we dusted it for prints, we'll find Larry's on it, not Jackson's."

"You will now," said Ryan. "After Larry helped take down Gerald's decorations."

"Why does it matter who turned off the electricity?" Warren asked.

Stan sighed, and Keya looked at him.

"Because it speaks of the credibility of the witness, or witnesses in this case," said Stan, sounding dejected. "If they lie about a small detail, what's to say they're telling the truth about the important ones, like how Bartholomew actually died?"

"Let's take a quick break," Keya suggested, standing up and stretching her arms back to release the tension in her shoulders. She rubbed her left arm and shoulder and was pleased to find there was no pain. But her neck was sore from leaning forward and staring at her computer screen.

Stan made hot drinks and returned with a plastic container of "Mrs Rowbottom's iced Christmas stars."

Keya crunched one, with white and green icing, as she considered what to raise next in the unravelling case of Bartholomew's death.

When everyone was seated again, Keya perched on her desk and said, "What if we relook at Bartholomew's death on the basis that the statements we, I, took are not entirely truthful?"

Stan said, "I think anything they said would be close to the truth, as I don't see them all making up and sticking to a fanciful story. We've already established that Larry wasn't able to keep to the one they devised, and I doubt Annie or Glenda would be able to stray too far from the facts."

"I don't like where this is going," voiced Ryan.

"I know," Keya agreed. "But I also know it's our job, and our moral duty, to present the facts and make our decisions based on them, and not on our personal feelings towards the victims or the suspects."

"Then this was a murder?" asked Warren.

"The facts," repeated Keya, "starting with the timeframe within which the death could, according to science, have occurred."

"Three-twenty to six-twenty," stated Sujin. "But we can reduce that as the ambulance crew reported the victim dead when they arrived at five-forty."

"Who called the ambulance?" asked Stan.

Keya double-checked her notes. "Gabrielle did at five-fifteen."

"She wouldn't call it until after Bartholomew fell, so we're down to between three-twenty and five-fifteen, until Warren can provide any footage or photos to narrow it further."

"So what I really need to find is video of our victim falling off the ladder?" Warren smiled.

Keya smiled back. "If one was out there, wouldn't it have gone viral by now? But there's no harm in looking." She didn't want to dampen his enthusiasm.

Then she arranged her face into a serious expression and said, "When I arrived, Warren was on crowd control and Inspector Evans was standing beside the body in the company of Larry and Jackson. Annie and Glenda were to one side, seemingly comforting each other. I escorted Glenda and Annie around the side of the house and into the kitchen diner by way of the back door. Glenda sat down and Annie started making tea, and they both appeared comfortable with that arrangement, even though it was Glenda's kitchen."

"Annie's good at that. Mothering people," Ryan commented.

"She, Annie that is, said Bartholomew had become obsessed by the inflatable Santa, which he could see while he worked. That may well be true, and it might be my fault for pointing it out when I interviewed him earlier in the day."

When none of the others made any comment, Keya continued, "Glenda blamed herself for not taking down the decorations. Then Gabrielle arrived, and I asked all three women what they thought had happened in respect of Bartholomew's 'accident'. Annie said she was at home, and Glenda was quick to add that she was with her."

Sujin picked up the cue and asked, "Do you think Glenda was lying about being at Annie's?"

"Possibly, because at that point, Annie knocked a mug off the countertop."

"In shock or surprise?" queried Sujin.

"Thinking back, it could have been either or both."

"But why would Glenda lie?" Ryan asked in an uncertain tone.

Keya sighed. "I have no idea, and after that, Gabrielle took over and spoke for all three women. She said she was at home, heard Bartholomew's cry and came to see what had happened. I presume Jackson was with her, but nobody has confirmed that."

Stan leaned forward in Inspector Evans' high-backed office chair and asked, "Did anyone see Bart during the afternoon?"

Keya admitted, "I don't actually know. And I've been searching for the inspector's notes, as he arrived in Glenda's kitchen and sent me out to help Sujin. I presumed he'd continued the interviews, but if he did, there's no record."

Looking at Ryan, Keya said, "We need to interview them all again. Separately so they can't cover for each other."

"Shame," Stan said. "They've had time to compose themselves and get their story straight."

"True. Perhaps I should call the inspector to find out what the women said, but I think we'll interview them again anyway," Keya reasoned.

"What would you like me to do?" asked Stan.

Keya considered Stan's question and thought through aspects of the investigation that still needed tackling. Then she replied, "Can you look into Glenda's background, and after that, Annie's, and both of the deceased? See if anything of note pops up."

She paused before adding, "And it might be best if you contact the inspector. Even if he didn't make a formal report, I'd like to know what the women told him after I left, and if there was anything in particular that struck him. But don't mention that we're re-evaluating the time of death."

"Why?" queried Stan.

"Because, at the moment," Keya replied, "we need to treat our former boss as an unreliable witness."

CHAPTER THIRTY-SEVEN

R yan drove himself and Keya to Limes Lane in a police car. This was an official visit, and Keya wanted their interviewees to know it. Larry looked over his hedge at them as they climbed out of the car.

Keya looked back at Ryan and said discreetly, "Why don't you interview Larry while I go and see Glenda?"

Keya thought Larry was more likely to open up to Ryan and Glenda to her. By splitting up, they could get through the interviews more quickly.

There were still no lights on in Annie's house as Keya walked up to Glenda's front door and rang the doorbell. Glenda answered, not quite concealing her irritation at seeing Keya again. As Keya was not officially on duty, she was wearing civilian clothes, but over the top, she'd added an official black police jacket.

"Keya," greeted Glenda uncertainly.

"May I come in?" asked Keya formally.

"Of course. Is this an official visit?"

Keya knew she needed to set the right tone. "Yes, it is. We still have a number of points to clear up regarding both your husband's and Bartholomew's deaths."

"Oh," Glenda responded noncommittally as she led Keya through to the kitchen diner, glancing at a clock on the wall as they entered. It was neat and tidy, with no splashes of milk on the countertop or broken crockery on the floor. An official-looking white envelope lay on one of the work surfaces.

Glenda leaned against the kitchen units as Keya asked, "I know you're fed up with our questions, but can we run through the events leading up to Gerald's death one final time so that I can fill in the blanks in our case notes before passing them over to the coroner's office?"

"So you're close to concluding his case?" Glenda sounded relieved.

"I believe we are, as I know you'd like closure before Christmas. Are you spending it here?"

"No, some friends from Bristol have invited me to celebrate with them. To be honest, I'll be pleased to get out of this house."

"Will you sell it?"

"I was considering staying, but now that…" Glenda caught herself. "After all that's happened, I think I'll move back to the city. Not that there's much there for me to look forward to. I'm unlikely to get my old job back, as they're laying off much younger staff than me. I'm not sure what I'll do."

Keya smiled empathetically. "On the day of Gerald's death, did anything unusual happen, or did you have any visitors?"

"No, I don't think so. The only visitors I have are my neighbours. Larry might have popped in to help with something, or Annie for a cup of tea. I can't remember, to be honest." She checked her wristwatch and glanced at the white envelope.

"Do you know when Gerald bought the elf decoration?"

Glenda sighed before responding. "It must have been online over the weekend. A parcel, which I presume was the elf, arrived on Monday morning and, as always with his Christmas decorations, he was as excited as a schoolboy. He even called me into his office that morning to show it to me."

"Did he mention anything about its power?"

"Power?" Glenda stared at her blankly.

"That it was battery-operated?"

"Oh, I see what you mean. The decorations often are, but Gerald converts most to mains electricity."

"How?" Keya asked, fishing to see how much detail Glenda knew.

"Instead of putting in batteries, he exposes the positive and negative terminals and attaches cables to them which run to a power adapter."

"It's something he's done often?"

"Oh, yes."

"So what do you think happened this time?"

"I've no idea. He must have run cables to the wrong terminals and shorted the circuit." Again, Glenda glanced at her watch.

Keya was impressed by the ease with which Glenda spoke about the technical terms. It was clear she did have knowledge of electrics, and, for the first time, Keya really looked at her.

Before, she'd seen a lonely woman whose husband had wanted to move to the country. Then, the grieving widow who was struggling to function. But gradually, that veneer had been scratched off, exposing a far more competent and capable woman. Could Glenda have orchestrated her husband's death?

"Where did Gerald do his work? In the study?" Keya asked.

"Yes, it was more of a workroom than an office. Tools and bits of plastic and wires were scattered around it. He was always tinkering with something."

"And where were you when Gerald died?"

"In the house, cooking supper. At least I was until the electricity cut out." Glenda answered Keya's questions without emotion.

Of course, this answer didn't mean much, as Glenda had ample opportunity to tamper with the elf before Gerald's death, and Keya thought she was quite capable of doing so.

Glenda glanced over Keya's head at the wall-mounted clock and shifted her weight from one foot to the other.

In her own mind, Keya had established that Glenda had the expertise to tamper with the illuminated elf that killed her husband, but short of a confession, she didn't see how she could prove that she had.

Even if Glenda's fingerprints were on the control box, she could claim she moved it when cleaning.

Unsure what further information she could glean from Glenda about her husband's death, Keya said, "Thank you. That was most helpful."

"When do you think Gerald's body will be released?"

"Hopefully next week. Will you hold a funeral?"

"I'm not sure who'll miss him, but I guess I'll put out a notice and invite people to the crematorium. I suspect it'll be a woefully attended event, but one I just need to get through."

Glenda didn't sound at all grief-stricken. Indeed, the whole process sounded more like an inconvenience to her. But perhaps it was just her way of coping.

It was time to move on and question Glenda about Bartholomew's death.

CHAPTER THIRTY-EIGHT

"Thank you, Glenda. That was really helpful. Now, we need to do the same regarding Bartholomew's death, so Annie can also have closure."

"Oh, of course," said Glenda, anxiously rubbing the back of her neck.

"Remind me of your movements on Monday afternoon," Keya said in a casual tone.

"Annie and I were having tea together here…" Glenda paused.

Keya didn't react, even though Glenda had already changed her story. But she did ask, "Did you see Bartholomew?"

"Yes, no. Well, I heard him shouting. Annie said he was in a mood because she'd forgotten to take him his three-thirty cup of tea. He was a real stickler for that sort of thing. Poor Annie, she was in such a state that she dropped the milk jug."

Keya remembered Annie wiping milk off the counter and the green pottery spout she'd picked up from Glenda's kitchen floor after Annie had dropped a mug. She couldn't help thinking that Bartholomew Beckett was a brute.

"Did you go outside when you heard him shout?"

"No, and neither did Annie. Bart could be nasty when he was angry. I think the term Annie used was a narcissist, but I think he was just a bully. And a social climber. Much good it did him, though. But he was too pig-headed to see when people were deliberately avoiding him."

"So you heard Bart shouting, and then you saw him carry Gerald's ladder past the window?"

"I couldn't believe…" Glenda began before catching herself.

"What? That he found the ladder? That he'd take it without asking? Or that he'd consider using it?"

Glenda drew her lips together and didn't respond.

Keya sighed. "Glenda, you need to be honest with me. We can't close this case and leave you all alone until we have everything resolved. And I think you and your friends have been far from truthful with me. So, I repeat, did you see Bartholomew carrying the ladder?"

"Yes," Glenda admitted contritely.

"And?" pressed Keya.

"Annie became agitated, asking us what we thought he was doing, that he might hurt himself. And, of course, he did."

Keya was about to ask another question when Glenda blurted, "And I'm not sorry he's dead. And Annie is free, and…" again Glenda's voice trailed off.

In a gentler tone, Keya asked, "Annie is free to do what?"

"Live her own life."

Keya felt a quiver in her stomach but pressed on. "I still need to speak to Annie. When did you last see her?"

"Not long ago," Glenda replied vaguely, with an edge of reluctance.

Keya was starting to feel irritated by Glenda's refusal to be upfront and open. "Not long ago today? Yesterday? Several days ago?"

Glenda drew her lips together before finally admitting, "It was earlier in the week. She said she had to go to London to put Bart's financial affairs in order."

"And did she say when she was coming back?"

"I think today. A package arrived for her this morning," Glenda glanced apprehensively at the white envelope resting on the countertop, "which she asked me to look out for and hold on to until she could pick it up."

"When you see her, please tell her I need to speak to her as a matter of urgency. Today, preferably. I'll pop back this afternoon and if she's still not around, again over the weekend. I'm under pressure to conclude these cases, and I can't do that without speaking to Annie."

"Why?" Glenda asked, pushing herself into a standing position. Her chin jutted out defiantly.

Keya raised her eyebrows. She had expected this response from Glenda. It was as if she was protecting Annie. But why did she feel she needed to?

"Because there are several points only she can clear up." Keya stared at Glenda, who stared back, her eyes narrowing.

Keya could feel Glenda's mind working as the other woman took a deep breath and nodded to herself. It was as if she'd made a decision. Keya waited, but Glenda remained silent.

The doorbell broke the charged atmosphere.

"That might be Annie now," Glenda said brightly as she walked past Keya.

Keya looked around the tidy room with a feeling that she'd overlooked something. But what?

"Is Keya still here?" she heard Ryan ask.

Shaking her head, Keya walked out of the kitchen diner. Ryan was standing on the other side of the open front door, smiling enquiringly.

"I'm here. And I think I'm finished. For now." She looked at Glenda.

"Pop back anytime," Glenda responded brightly, with no hint of irritation. But was there an undertone of relief?

As Keya walked down the garden path, mulling over her interview with Glenda, Ryan asked, "What's up?"

She stopped and turned back to the house. The front door was closed, and the house stood innocently in front of her. A house where two men had died. She shivered.

"I don't know. I think it's this case. And the feeling that something else is going on, but I can't see what it is."

"You don't think Bart was a drug dealer or Gerald an international fugitive?" Ryan joked.

"No." Keya smiled and turned away from the house. Perhaps

taking responsibility for a case after being on sick leave for so long was too much for her. Was she trying too hard or missing signs she'd normally pick up?

But the uneasy feeling in her stomach was still there.

Ignoring it, she asked, "Did you find out anything from Larry?"

"Yes, he said..."

Keya cut in. "Actually, don't tell me now. We should report back to the whole team." Because she didn't trust herself?

"What about Annie? And Jackson and Gabrielle?"

"Let's try Annie's door, but I don't think she's there. Glenda finally admitted that she's gone to London to sort out Bart's affairs, and she'll be back today."

Sure enough, there was no answer at Annie's house.

When they rang Gabrielle and Jackson's doorbell, they only heard Chief barking.

"No point hanging around here. Let's grab some sandwiches for the team on the way back and eat them while we go over what we've all learned this morning."

As Ryan drove out of Limes Lane, Keya stared at the motorcyclist who turned in and passed them.

CHAPTER THIRTY-NINE

B ack at Cirencester Police Station, Stan handed out drinks while
Ryan offered everyone sandwiches from the selection they'd
bought at a supermarket before returning to the station.

Keya sat behind her desk and clenched her hands. Why did she feel
so agitated and uptight?

"Falafel and hummus wrap," said Ryan, placing a plastic packet on
her desk.

She ignored it. What was troubling her? Something about her
interview with Glenda this morning. The feeling that Glenda had been
waiting for something. She'd been constantly looking at her watch or
glancing at the clock on the wall.

She hadn't exactly told Keya to leave, but she hadn't been
particularly welcoming. Perhaps she wasn't a natural hostess. But at
least Keya would have expected her to offer her a cup of tea.

She picked up the mug Stan had placed on her desk and sipped it.

What would make Glenda uptight? They'd established that she
didn't have any friends locally, apart from her neighbours.

Looking up, Keya asked, "Stan, what did you find out about
Glenda?"

"She'd worked for the same company for fifteen years as a junior
lab assistant, moving to senior lab assistant. She wasn't ambitious but

appeared to enjoy her job and the people she worked with. I spoke to her former boss, and although he was sorry to see her go, as she was very competent, he's had to lay off several members of staff during the last few months due to budget cuts."

"Has he seen her since she left?"

"Not in person, although she did inquire about returning to work."

"And?"

"Her boss sounded sorry but said there wasn't anything he could offer her. But I did ask him if she had any knowledge of electrics, and he said she'd certainly know her way around a circuit board."

"So that's a yes?"

"I'd say so," agreed Stan.

Keya tapped her fingers on her desk.

Ryan, who was sitting opposite her, said, "Shall I tell you about my talk with Larry now?"

"Yes. When Sujin gets here."

"I'm here," Sujin said, walking into the room.

"Roast beef and horseradish OK for you?" Ryan asked, holding up a triangular cardboard packet of sandwiches.

"Thanks," Sujin said, taking them from Ryan and sitting down behind the desk next to him. Warren was seated at the desk beside Keya, and Stan sat in the inspector's chair in the doorway to the empty office. Keya took a breath, trying to calm her racing pulse and overactive brain.

"Go ahead," she said to Ryan.

"Larry was definitely hiding something. And he couldn't keep his story straight. I really thought he'd open up to me, but he wouldn't, which surprised me. I'd say he was telling the truth when he said he saw the others gathering in Glenda's garden and went to see what was happening, and that he turned off the electricity before letting anyone touch Bart."

"Did he say anything about the giant Santa?" Keya asked.

"No, and I didn't prompt him. After what you suggested, I did think it interesting and important that he omitted to say anything about the inflatable decoration. He did confirm that Bart was lying on the grass and the ladder was propped up against the wall."

"That, at least, I think is truthful," accepted Keya. "Did he say exactly who was there?"

"No, he just referred to 'everyone'."

"And what about the timing?"

"That's when he became particularly vague, providing only single-word answers."

"As if he didn't want to let anything slip?"

"Exactly."

Keya sighed.

"I have some news," Sujin announced. "But I don't think you're going to like it."

"Don't tell me. You isolated Annie's fingerprints and they were the missing ones on the ladder," replied Keya in a resigned voice.

"Er, yes. How did you know that?"

Keya sat up. "I didn't. Or at least not consciously. Go on."

"I sketched out the ladder and where the prints were positioned, and hers are on the side like this." Sujin held his arms out, shoulder-width apart. "As if she was gripping the ladder."

"As if she was gripping the ladder," repeated Keya. One penny fell into place.

"And the Santa?" inquired Keya.

"That had Jackson and Glenda's prints on it. I suppose it's not a surprise Glenda's were there, but Jackson's?"

Another penny fell into place.

"He'd leave his prints if he moved the Santa. Like placing it over Bartholomew's body to hide it from view."

"The inspector did confirm the Santa was lying on the body when he arrived at the scene," Stan said.

"You spoke to him?" Keya didn't know why this surprised her.

"Yes, although it wasn't always easy to hear what he said. I think he was driving."

"Did he say who called him to the scene?"

"Er, no. And I didn't ask."

Keya had her suspicions, but she'd let it go for the moment. "What else did he say?"

"He confirmed that our report of what happened after he arrived is correct."

"And the interview with the women after I went to help Sujin?"

"Ah, that's when he started to break up. But I think he said he didn't learn an awful lot. They comforted Annie, and Glenda offered to sleep at Annie's house to keep her company if she didn't want to be alone."

"And that was it?"

"Almost." Stan drew his eyebrows together.

"What is it?" Keya asked.

"If I hadn't been calling him about the case, I'd have said we were having a totally different conversation. He told me to look after Mrs Rowbottom, and to think about taking retirement and spending some time together. It was strange really, but maybe he's just had time to think about life and his priorities since he quit his job."

"And decided to move to Australia," Keya added.

Another penny dropped.

Sharply, she asked, "Did he say anything else?"

"Well, yes, he did." Again, Stan drew his eyebrows together, and he pursed his lips as he regarded Keya.

"He apologised to you. He said, 'Tell Keya I'm sorry, but I hope she understands. And it's nothing personal, but this time I have to do what is morally right, even if it isn't considered legally right.' I don't know what he meant by that."

Keya jumped to her feet.

"I have to go."

"Don't you want to hear about my findings?" asked Warren anxiously.

"No time," blurted Keya.

"Hear him out," said Stan calmly. "Where angels tread and all that."

Keya took a deep breath, but her heart was still racing as she slumped back into her chair.

"What did you discover?" Stan asked Warren.

"The earliest video I found was timed at half past four, and there was no inflatable Santa on the side of the house. But I was able to zoom in and see the ladder. And I think there was a figure standing beside it, but I need Sujin or Ryan's expertise to work out who it is."

The final penny fell, and Keya jumped up again, her head clearer.

"Ryan, come with me. Sujin, can you and Warren work on that video footage? Stan, see if you can find the inspector. You might need to check the airlines and flights to Australia today."

"What?" Stan sounded incredulous.

"I think you were right about your call with the inspector, and it was his way of saying goodbye."

CHAPTER FORTY

"Put your foot down," Keya instructed as she clicked a switch, and the police siren sounded. Ryan glanced at her before gripping the steering wheel and swerving around the traffic in front of him, which was trying its best to move out of their way.

"Why the rush?" he called, narrowly missing a wobbling cyclist.

"Because I think the turkey has already escaped the pen."

"You mean the chicken has flown the coop?" Ryan corrected.

"I mean, we're going to be too late, and it's my fault. I should have figured out what was going on this morning when I visited Glenda."

"Which is?"

"Just concentrate on driving."

Ryan skidded into Limes Lane and braked sharply to a halt behind a silver Volvo SUV. The chief constable's wife, who was removing a box containing oranges wrapped in red ribbons, stared as Keya and Ryan dashed past her and up Annie's garden path.

"Try the bell," Keya instructed as she ran round the side of the house, looking for an open window. But it was a cold winter's day, and all the windows were tightly shut.

"No answer," said Ryan when she returned.

"A key. There must be one somewhere."

Keya searched under the plant pots until she heard Ryan shout, "There's a key box here!"

She joined him round the other side of the house, next to the enclosure that hid the dustbins from sight.

"Any idea what the code is?"

"No, but people don't usually click the numbers too far around. Let me see if I can work it out."

"You do that. I want a word with Glenda. I think she knows exactly where Annie is." Keya strode out of the rear gate and round to Glenda's back door, which she rapped on sharply.

She waited impatiently until Glenda opened the door, a sardonic smile on her face. "Back so soon, Keya?"

"Where's Annie?"

"I'm afraid you've missed her."

"You do know the UK has an extradition agreement with Australia. And I can arrest you for perverting the course of justice and attempting to cover up and conceal a crime?"

Although Glenda just stared at her, Keya had the feeling that she was thinking through her options. Good, she might decide it was time to tell the truth.

"Come in," Glenda replied.

Keya stepped through the back door and glanced at the boots and shoes in the utility room, which were now arranged in a neat line. There seemed far fewer than she remembered, and Glenda must already have started clearing out Gerald's things.

This time, Glenda did switch the kettle on and reached into a cupboard for two mugs while keeping her back to Keya.

Both women remained silent.

When the kettle had finished whistling and switched itself off, and Glenda had poured hot water into a green teapot, she finally turned to face Keya. She was no longer smiling, and her eyes were dull.

She sighed as she poured two cups of tea and, as she handed one to Keya, she appeared to make a decision.

"I'm not sure why you're so concerned about Annie. I told you, she hasn't done anything wrong," Glenda stated.

"I need to speak to her in connection with her husband's death."

"Because you think she had something to do with it?"

"The evidence points that way."

"What evidence?"

"Her fingerprints are on the ladder, indicating that she was holding it when Bartholomew climbed up. And there is video footage from one of the visitors to Gerald's lights, showing her standing next to it." Keya knew this hadn't been proved, but she expected it was Annie on the video Warren had found.

A flicker of annoyance crossed Glenda's face as she spat, "Gerald and his infernal lights!" She sipped her tea, composed herself, and said in a defensive tone, "I don't see what that proves."

"It means the statement Annie gave, that you all gave, is false. You were lying. Annie was in the garden with Bartholomew when he climbed the ladder."

"I can assure you, she was not."

"OK, then she went out when he'd already climbed up, but either way, it appears that she was responsible for her husband's death."

"I was under the impression that he died as a result of falling off the ladder."

"Which Annie might have caused."

"Might have?"

Keya ploughed on, ignoring Glenda's sceptical tone. "And there was another head wound which can't be accounted for, with a clean cut."

"Ah, that'll be from where I hit him with the milk jug."

Keya blinked. "You did what?"

"He was in my kitchen ranting and raving at Annie, all because she'd forgotten to take him his afternoon cup of tea. You'd have thought it was the end of the world. I had to shut him up somehow, so I picked the milk jug up off the counter and whacked him over the side of the head with it. It wasn't the best thing I could have chosen, but at least it was nearly empty."

"So you admit to striking Bartholomew?"

"Yes, I do. Annie didn't deserve a husband like that. None of us do. When you marry someone, you expect a partnership with mutual respect and understanding, and you envision spending quality time together. Don't you forget that."

"Are you talking about Annie or yourself?"

"Both, I suppose," Glenda admitted, as she glanced down at her feet.

Keya waited for Glenda to continue.

Glenda looked up and, holding eye contact with Keya, announced, "It was me. I killed Bart."

"No, you didn't," countered Keya.

"And I killed Gerald, although I didn't mean to."

"That I do accept. You had the knowledge and the opportunity to tamper with the lighting control box."

"True, but I only meant to give him a little shock and for the lights to go out. I was so sick of them, and of people coming to stare at the house night after night. Why couldn't he be normal? We could have gone to see the Christmas lights together in Cheltenham or Bristol, but no, he had to create his own display."

"So when the new elf light arrived, and you saw it on his worktable, and that he was converting it to mains power…"

"I rewired it," Glenda said, still maintaining eye contact.

"But you were in your kitchen when Bartholomew fell from the ladder."

"No, I was in the garden."

"With Annie?"

"Yes, I admit, she was there."

"And she grabbed the ladder because her husband was trying to take down Gerald's decorations, and she knew it wasn't his place and that he might hurt himself," proposed Keya.

"That's right, she was concerned about his safety," replied Glenda levelly.

Silently, Keya remonstrated with herself for putting words into Glenda's mouth and for offering Annie a way out.

She ploughed on. "Annie grabbed the ladder. Maybe she didn't mean to shake it, but Bartholomew wouldn't be the most stable person on it, and the movement caused him to fall."

"Annie did grab the ladder, but only out of concern. I pushed her aside, and I was the one who shouted at Bart to come down. And I shook the ladder to let him know I was serious. It hardly moved, but Bart was stretching out to unhook the Santa, and I just watched as he and the giant red inflatable fell to the ground together. The Santa bounced away, but Bart didn't. He just lay on the ground, clutching the electric cable."

"And that was why Larry suggested turning off the electricity before touching him?"

"I had to grab Annie to stop her, and she kept calling Bart's name, but even before Larry turned off the power at the fuse box, it was clear Bart was dead."

"What I don't understand is why you didn't call an ambulance straight away. Why wait?"

Glenda shrugged. "He was dead. What harm was there in waiting an hour or so?"

She didn't add, 'so we could get our story straight and calm Annie down,' but Keya had no doubt that was the real reason.

"And Annie had nothing to do with her husband's death," Keya pressed.

"She did not," Glenda replied emphatically.

"Keya," called Ryan. "I opened the box and used the key to access Annie's house. She's not there. Actually, I don't think she's coming back."

Glenda smiled. No, she smirked.

Keya stared at Glenda as she shouted back, "She's not! She and Inspector Evans have left for Australia. Hopefully, Stan will catch them before they depart. Then I can hear Annie's side of the story."

Glenda glanced at the clock on the wall behind Keya. "I don't think that'll be happening."

Keya pressed her lips together but tried to hide her disappointment. "I presume the package that arrived for Annie today was her passport. But I don't see how she had time to collect it, get to the airport, and fly."

"I did lie to you about one thing. I wasn't expecting Annie back today. She stayed up in London, and a motorbike courier collected her passport."

Keya groaned. The motorcyclist she and Ryan had passed entering Limes Lane after their morning interviews.

She turned and walked to the back door, where Ryan stood waiting for her. She said, "Call Stan. See if he's located the inspector."

Glenda regarded Keya as she re-entered the kitchen and said, "You do understand, don't you?"

Keya didn't respond, but grudgingly, she thought she did.

Glenda hadn't wanted to leave her life in Bristol, but she'd followed her husband to Cirencester, where his passion for Christmas lights had turned into an obsession.

His display had irritated his neighbour, Bartholomew, who complained about the visitors and the effect on house prices. And both men had been annoyed by the disturbance of Jackson's parties.

While the men in the recently constructed houses were at odds with each other, and with Larry and his unsightly property opposite them, the women had banded together and befriended each other and Larry.

At some point, Glenda must have decided she'd finally had enough of the lights and realised that the lead-up to Christmas would become increasingly fraught and fractious as more and more visitors turned up outside their house.

As the council had been unwilling or unable to do anything about the spectacle, Glenda had taken matters into her own hands.

"Why didn't you tamper with the lights already in the garden or on the house?" asked Keya. It was what Larry said he'd have done.

"Because Gerald would have pottered about and calmly fixed them."

But would he have done the same with a new light? Keya wondered. And had Glenda only meant to give him a shock? Surely, she'd have known the potentially fatal consequences of tampering with the control box.

Keya looked up at Glenda, who was watching her calmly. She realised Glenda probably did, but doubted she would admit it.

And then there was lovely, friendly Annie with her bullying husband. Keya could understand why that would incense Glenda. Perhaps Glenda hadn't meant to shake him off the ladder. Then again, maybe she hadn't been anywhere near it, and it was Annie who'd caused her husband's fall.

What had the inspector told Stan? 'Tell Keya I'm sorry, and I need to do what is morally right.'

Did he know what Annie had done? And why? And he'd covered it up?

Meanwhile, there was Glenda, with seemingly nothing to lose, admitting to both crimes. She'd probably only get a few years added to her sentence for Bartholomew's death, but that hardly mattered.

A life sentence for killing her husband was just that—life imprisonment. What did an additional sentence matter? She couldn't serve time beyond the end of her life.

Ryan stepped into the kitchen, stuffing his phone into his jacket pocket. "The inspector and Annie Beckett left on a flight to Sydney, Australia, an hour ago."

Glenda smiled and leaned back against the kitchen units. "They did it."

"Glenda Sadler," began Keya in her professional voice, "I'm arresting you for the murder of Gerald Sadler and for the manslaughter of Bartholomew Beckett."

Beside her, Ryan gasped.

Keya continued, "You do not have to say anything, but it may harm your defence if you do not mention when questioned something you later rely on in court."

CHAPTER FORTY-ONE

K eya stood in the queue in the custody suite of Cirencester Police Station, with Glenda standing calmly beside her.

At the desk, a woman swore at the custody sergeant and claimed she had no idea how a pair of EarPods and a smartwatch ended up in her bag. After several minutes, a uniformed constable escorted the woman away.

"Yes, Keya," said the custody sergeant.

Keya said in a clear, professional voice, "Sergeant Keya Varma. I arrested Glenda Sadler at 14:40 at Limes Lane, Stratton, Cirencester, on suspicion of the murder of her husband, Gerald Sadler, and the manslaughter of Bartholomew Beckett."

Keya was aware of Sujin stepping out of his workroom to watch the proceedings.

"Thank you, Sergeant, we'll take matters from here. Do you have legal representation?" the duty sergeant asked Glenda.

"No," she replied calmly.

"Would you like me to contact the duty solicitor?"

"Yes, please."

"While we await their arrival, you will be processed and seen by the duty nurse. Do you understand?"

When another constable arrived to take over responsibility for

Glenda, Keya moved to stand beside Sujin. As they watched Glenda being led away, Sujin said, "I think you'll need to explain this one over supper. But in the meantime, is there anything you need me to do?"

"Yes," Keya began, but then she caught herself.

Was it really in the public interest to continue investigating the case? To try to prove Glenda wasn't responsible for Bartholomew's death and that Annie was. How much time would it take Sujin to try to prove this? And at what cost?

Could they ever conclusively prove it wasn't Glenda? And who would challenge her confession?

In Glenda's eyes, Annie had suffered enough. What had she said? That Annie deserved to be free and start a new life.

And who better to look after her and keep her on the straight and narrow than Inspector Evans? What effect would all this have on Annie? Would she be consumed by guilt?

Keya sighed. There wasn't anything she could do. She turned to Sujin and said, "No, I don't think there's anything you can do at the moment. And supper would be great, but not too late. I'm exhausted by this case."

She felt her phone vibrate. Removing it from her pocket, she read the new message.

"It's from Maitri," she told Sujin. "Reminding me I promised to help her with an apprenticeship application."

"Apprenticeship. That sounds like a good idea. On-the-job training."

"Yes, but I doubt it will be at the cafe," Keya replied, before stopping herself. She didn't want to hold her youngest sister back, as she had the whole of her life ahead of her. "I better go and help her."

As Keya stepped out of her car in front of the antique centre, a snowflake landed on her nose. Inside, the cafe was buzzing, and for a moment she froze in the doorway, feeling disoriented.

It was such a different world from the one she'd inhabited this morning. Or was it?

Looking around at the many varied expressions on her customers' faces, she considered that she had no idea what crimes or actions any of them had committed or might commit in the future.

It was the normal, everyday people, and the actions they were pushed into taking, that still shocked and surprised her.

She realised she was echoing Ryan's thoughts and one of the reasons why he was looking for another job, whatever that was.

"Hi," greeted Zivah, who looked happy despite the black bags under her eyes. "A parcel arrived for you earlier."

"It did?"

"Yes, I gave it to Norman to look after."

Keya crossed the cafe, greeting her regular customers in as upbeat a manner as she could muster.

"Hi, Keya," Norman said. "We heard back on the planning consent."

"Good or bad news?"

"Not great, I'm afraid, but…"

"Sorry," Keya interrupted. "It's been a stressful day. Can you tell me about it later?"

"Of course." Norman smiled sympathetically. "What you need is a special festive hot chocolate."

Keya wasn't sure she did, but she smiled gratefully and asked, "Do you know where my parcel is?"

"I kept it safe for you." Norman reached down behind his counter and reemerged with a brown cardboard box. Keya's name and the address of the cafe were printed in large black letters.

Picking up a knife, she carried the parcel to a spare table and cut the tape binding it.

Inside were two white envelopes and something wrapped in tissue paper, nestling in scrunched-up newspaper.

She opened the smaller envelope and removed a card with a typical Cotswolds scene on the front. Houses constructed of honey-coloured stone, set in gardens full of colourful flowers located beside a stream.

Inside was a handwritten note.

Dear Keya,

I'm sorry I can't say goodbye in person, but by now you'll probably have worked out why. I spoke to the chief inspector and realised you wouldn't give up on the Limes Lane cases. But then, I've trained you well!

Please leave this one be. It'll be best for all of us. I'll keep an eye on Annie as we start our new life together. I hope you understand, and that you can forgive us both and wish us happiness in our new venture together.

I'm not coming back, whatever happens, as I know I crossed a line. Which is why I've left you a parting gift. Keep it or sell it, that's up to you. But I'd like to think you'll keep it, redecorate, and make it your own so that you and Sujin will be happy there, just as I was with Mother.

I've included something for Stan, Ryan, Beanie, and Dotty for when you next see her. I'd be grateful if you could make sure they all receive their gifts. I've also enclosed something for you to remember me by, if you wish.

And if you and Sujin fancy a honeymoon in Australia, Annie's and my home will always be open to you.

With a sorrowful heart, but looking to a bright future,
Dai Evans

Keya felt tears prick her eyes, and she wiped them away with the back of her hand as Millie placed a red mug of hot chocolate topped with whipped cream, mini marshmallows, and a segment of chocolate orange in front of her.

"Are you OK?" Millie asked in a concerned voice.

"I will be. I'm just having a moment." Keya smiled sadly up at Millie.

"Then I'll leave you be, but call if you need anything."

Going over the inspector's words in her head, she took out the tissue-wrapped package and carefully opened it.

Smiling sadly, she stared at a framed photograph of herself with the inspector, Ryan, their old colleague Nick, and her friend Dotty outside Windrush Hall. It must have been taken after they'd successfully solved another case together.

She reached into the box and removed the larger envelope, noting several smaller ones lying beneath it. The top one had Stan's name printed on it.

Opening the end of the large envelope, she reached in and pulled out a cream-coloured document. Several sheets of paper fell onto the table.

Her breath caught in her throat as she stared at the front page. It was the deed to the inspector's house in Tetbury.

So that's what he'd meant about her and Sujin being happy there together. He'd given her his house, presuming she and Sujin would stay together, maybe even get married, since he'd invited them to Australia for their honeymoon.

But his house? The double-fronted stone cottage with the retro kitchen and 1960s and 1970s decor.

Was it too much? Was it a bribe for not pursuing Annie's case? Or was it a generous gift from a friend who had nobody else to leave it to and knew she wouldn't have the heart to sell it?

She smiled, knowing it was the latter, and plucked the melting segment of chocolate orange from her hot chocolate, licking the whipped cream off it.

"Not like you to be staring into space, but that hot chocolate does look delicious," Aunt Beanie's voice rang out.

Keya blinked and looked up at the older woman.

"Are you alright?" Aunt Beanie asked, sounding concerned. "Your face is blotchy. You've been crying!"

Sniffing, Keya replied, "I have something for you." She reached into the box and removed an envelope with Aunt Beanie's name on it, which she held up.

"A Christmas card, how lovely. I'm afraid I haven't written all mine yet," Aunt Beanie said apologetically.

"It's not a Christmas card, and it's not from me. And I recommend you open it now, before everyone knows the news."

"What news?" asked Aunt Beanie, her eyes narrowing as she pulled out a chair and sat down.

"Read that first."

Keya stirred her hot chocolate as Aunt Beanie tore open the

envelope and removed the card inside. Keya saw that it had a picture of a garden on the front.

"No!" exclaimed Aunt Beanie. "I don't believe it." And after a pause, "Such a shame, but so kind."

She placed the card on the table, and Keya noticed she also had a tear in her eye as she said, "He says I can take cuttings from the garden if you don't mind, as his mum loved being part of the gardening club with me."

"What garden?" Keya asked.

"Oh, haven't you seen it? There's a lovely garden at the back of the house in Tetbury. His mother spent hours tending to it."

"I had no idea."

"Well, it will be yours to work on, or so I understand."

"He told you about leaving his house to me?" Keya asked.

"He did. So now you need to tell me what's been going on and why Dai Evans has left for the other side of the world without even saying a proper goodbye."

Keya sat back and started to tell Aunt Beanie about the events of the past couple of weeks.

Partway through her tale, Norman brought Aunt Beanie a cup of tea and sat down to hear the end of the story.

"In a way," declared Aunt Beanie when Keya had finished, "I'm delighted for him. He deserves the love of a good woman."

CHAPTER FORTY-TWO

Keya, Aunt Beanie, and Norman raised their glasses to toast Inspector Dai Evans, wishing him well in his new life in South Australia.

Keya would certainly miss her gruff, sometimes grumpy boss. She was still struggling to come to terms with him whisking away a potential suspect, even though Glenda had now given a full and clear account of Bartholomew's death.

Keya believed that Glenda had hit him on the head with the milk jug. But Glenda had retracted her confession about shaking the ladder, insisting that neither she nor Annie caused Bartholomew to fall.

If that was true, why had the inspector and Annie needed to flee? Was it to spare Annie from hours of questioning and speculation about her involvement? Or did the inspector believe that, in the rush to wrap the case up before Christmas, Annie would be blamed, even though she wasn't involved?

Perhaps, one day, Keya would be able to get the full story from the inspector. But for now, she wiped a stray tear from her eye, turned to Norman, and said, "You were going to tell me about the planning consent."

"Don't mention that," Aunt Beanie declared loudly, and then continued, "Can you believe it? The conditions have been amended so that the barn can only be used for an agricultural or related purpose. How ridiculous. Poor Dotty. Antiques definitely don't fall into that bracket unless she only wants to sell old plough brasses, bits of rotting horse tack, or stone troughs."

"She's due back soon, isn't she?"

"Yes, this weekend, weather permitting," replied Aunt Beanie. "The snow is settling outside. But hopefully, she'll be here in time to help with Thursday's special festive auction."

"It'll be very festive if the snow continues," Norman remarked.

"Now I must collect the afternoon tea I ordered and deliver it to the nursing home for Cliff and Edith," Aunt Beanie said in a businesslike tone.

"How is Uncle Cliff?" Keya asked.

"Hanging on in there, but I'm not sure he'll make it much beyond the New Year. That's why I want this Christmas to be a special one. You are coming on Christmas Day?"

"Actually, Sujin and I are spending it at Zivah's house," replied Keya, feeling guilty.

"How lovely, with a baby in the house. And that means I can ask Mick. Monica said he's going to be on his own, and we can't have that."

Aunt Beanie stood up and walked away. As Norman pushed his chair back, he asked, "Are you sure you're alright?"

Keya nodded. "I will be, and thank you for the hot chocolate. It was delicious."

Maitri appeared at the table and said, "Do you mind if we postpone our apprenticeship chat? I've just received a delivery for the hamper orders, and I'm really excited to see what we have."

"That's fine. I'm not really feeling up to it at the moment. But how many orders do you have?"

"Lots, so I need to start putting them all together." Smiling, Maitri left Keya on her own.

Keya's phone buzzed. It was Ryan.

"Hi, I'm not sure how keen you are to return to Limes Lane, and even though Glenda has been arrested, I promised Larry I'd help take down the sleigh and reindeer from on top of Glenda's roof. Do you want to meet me there?"

Keya wasn't sure she did, but she should search Glenda's house, and it was probably better to do so now than next week.

"Yes, I'll see you there."

Back at Limes Lane, where a thin layer of snow covered the ground, Keya parked her car and watched Larry carry Gerald's ladder round to the front of the house, where he propped it up. Ryan tapped on Keya's window, and she nodded, picked up the inspector's envelope, which had Ryan's name on it, and opened the door.

"This is for you. From the inspector," Keya said as she joined Ryan at Glenda's garden gate.

"He's really gone?" asked Ryan, as if he couldn't quite believe it.

"He has, and he's left me his house!"

Ryan's eyes bulged.

"Open your envelope and see what he has to say to you."

Ryan tore his envelope open. Keya didn't see the image on the front of the card, but she heard Ryan gasp.

"Apparently, the inspector has a large coin collection, which he's giving to me. He said he's left it in the dining room." Ryan looked up at Keya and said, "I don't know what to say."

"Send him a letter or a postcard. I think he'd appreciate that more than an email."

Ryan nodded. "You're right."

"Are you two coming?" Larry called.

Ryan crossed to the ladder and held it while Larry climbed up. Keya pulled on a pair of latex gloves and entered Glenda's house.

The study was clean and tidy, although Gerald's toolbox was still on the table. They might be able to get Glenda's fingerprints from some of the tools, although there probably wasn't much point as she could claim she'd touched them while cleaning or tidying them away.

In the kitchen, Keya found a shard of green pottery and remembered the piece she'd picked up after Bartholomew's death, which had been from the spout of a jug. The milk jug which Glenda claimed she'd hit Bartholomew with.

The most interesting find was a pair of men's shoes in the now tidy utility room. They looked expensive and were highly polished, and the size didn't match either of the pairs of wellies.

Remembering Sujin's comment at the scene about Bartholomew wearing slippers, Keya bagged the shoes, wondering if Annie or Glenda had swapped them, though she couldn't understand why they would. But if they did belong to the victim, the fact they'd been found in Glenda's house provided more evidence against her.

With a final sigh, Keya left the house and found Gabrielle distracting Ryan as he held the ladder.

Stepping back, Keya watched Larry perform a precarious manoeuvre on the slippery, snow-covered roof. She wanted to shout out to him to be careful but decided against it. She didn't want to surprise him and have another body to deal with.

"I hear you've arrested Glenda, and she's confessed to both crimes," gushed Gabrielle.

Keya looked at Ryan, whose cheeks flushed as he concentrated hard on holding the ladder.

"I'm so excited. I've called my agent, and we've scheduled filming for next week. I hope the snow stays as it'll add to the atmosphere. I tried to persuade Larry to leave the reindeer and sleigh up on the roof, but he refused. Still, we have plenty of footage of the lights and the house."

Keya's mind wandered as Gabrielle continued outlining her plans. Why were people so fascinated by true crime shows? Was it because, deep down, many were only a short step away from being pushed into committing a serious crime themselves?

Her phone vibrated in her pocket, and she heard another phone ring. Ryan looked uncertain as he was still gripping the ladder.

"Hello?" Keya said.

"It's Stan. You and Ryan need to get yourselves back here now. The chief constable is arriving in half an hour."

CHAPTER FORTY-THREE

Keya and Ryan joined their colleagues, who were already gathered in the room on the first floor of Cirencester Police Station, where Chief Inspector Greg usually held his Friday coffee and chats.

But this was no informal gathering, and the atmosphere was tense as everyone waited for the chief constable.

Someone by the door called, "He's coming," and the attending officers and ancillary staff parted to allow the chief constable to stride to the front of the room.

"Thank you all for joining me on this wintry day. Firstly, I'd like to say how proud I am of you all and the professional manner in which you dealt with the review team and the uncertainty surrounding the future of your station. As you know, Cirencester Station will remain open under the direction and guidance of Chief Inspector Greg."

The chief constable paused, appearing to wait for a response, but as this was old news, he didn't receive one.

Continuing, he said, "But there will be some changes. Despite their recent and continuing success in solving crimes, the serious crime team will be merged with the murder squad in Gloucester."

Keya groaned, even though it was the news she'd been expecting.

"I am pleased to announce that Sujin Kerr has been promoted to the role of Regional Forensics Liaison Officer. He will oversee the integration of forensics and traditional police investigations in major crimes across the region."

There was polite clapping, and several officers close to Sujin said, "Congratulations."

"And recently promoted Sergeant Ryan Jenkins will also be leaving the team as he has secured a position as an Intelligence Officer in the National Crime Agency based in Bristol."

The response to this news was louder, with clapping and cheering, and several people clapped Ryan on the back. So that's what all the secrecy had been about. But why hadn't Ryan told her the news himself?

"And finally, it's time to really say goodbye to Stan Rowbottom, who has decided, this time, he really will take retirement."

What? This was news to Keya.

The chief constable continued, "After a long career in uniform and a shorter, though no less valuable, role in archives, and as an unofficial member of the serious crimes team, Stan has decided to spend more time with his family and do some travelling."

Keya glanced at Stan, and he winked back at her.

"And finally, you may be aware that Inspector Evans left suddenly. Anticipating that his team would be moved to headquarters, he searched for an alternative role and found one, of all places, in South Australia. I'm sure the police there will appreciate his expertise and strong work ethic."

There were a few sniggers, and the chief constable gave a wry smile before continuing to tell those assembled about the plans for the station. Partway through this, Keya tuned out.

There was polite applause when the chief constable finished his presentation and was escorted out of the room by Chief Inspector Greg.

As the room emptied, Keya turned to Ryan and asked, "Why didn't you tell me you'd landed your new job?"

"Because I didn't know I had. I've been waiting to hear back from the NCA."

"Well, I think we should celebrate," Stan said.

"Or commiserate," muttered Keya.

"What? Don't you want to wish me luck for my life beyond the police force?"

Keya smiled at Stan.

"And I want to hear all about your plans for the inspector's house."

As they descended the stairs, Chief Inspector Greg called, "Keya, can I have a word?"

Stan raised his eyebrows and said, "We'll ask Sujin to join us and meet you in the team room."

"Yes, sir," Keya said as she approached Chief Inspector Greg.

"I'm sorry about your team, especially after the excellent job you did leading them and tying up the cases on Limes Lane. And I realise you're in a difficult position, as you're still officially on sick leave. But Sujin told me about your application to attend the crime scene manager's course, and I've spoken to the organisers and told them of your recent work, and they've agreed to give you a place on the course, starting in January."

"Thank you, sir."

"I guess that means you'll also be leaving us?"

"There really isn't a place for me here now."

"It's the end of an era. I'll miss the inspector, despite all his foibles, and your team. It will be a much duller place without you."

CHAPTER FORTY-FOUR

Although the café was closed to customers the following Monday, Keya had agreed to help Maitri, Monica, and Mick prepare hampers and Christmas orders.

They were joined by Millie, Ryan, and Sujin. Millie insisted on playing Christmas tunes and conducting the group as they all sang Jingle Bells.

After the stresses and uncertainties of the previous week, Keya was pleased to get into the Christmas spirit. "We visited the inspector's house yesterday and collected the coins he left you," Keya told Ryan.

"That really was kind of him," Monica said as she rolled fondant icing onto a blue silicone mat on one of the café tables.

"What's the house like?" Millie asked.

"Dated, but with heaps of potential. Sujin suggested we knock the kitchen and dining room together to create a single, more spacious room. And we could install a pair of French windows to provide access to the lovely garden."

"So you're making plans together?" Millie teased.

Keya glanced at Sujin before answering, knowing she was blushing. "I'm going to move in straight after Christmas, as my place is still not habitable. And…" her voice trailed off, and she looked at Sujin again.

Sujin smiled and said, "And I'm giving notice on my house and moving in at the end of January."

Keya felt her face flush.

"You didn't tell me that, sis." Maitri gave Keya a friendly nudge on the arm with her elbow.

"We haven't told anyone. In fact, I didn't know if Sujin would agree to the proposal until last night."

Sujin stood back, hands on his hips. "I thought you were dragging your heels and wanted the place all to yourself." He laughed mischievously as Rockin' Around the Christmas Tree played.

Maitri grabbed Sujin's arm and made him dance with her beside the second Christmas tree they had set up near Norman's drinks counter. The number of gingerbread decorations had been too much for their first tree and the one Gilly had put up in the antique centre.

Mick smiled, and Keya remembered that this would be his first Christmas out of prison for a long time. She asked tentatively, "What are you doing for Christmas?"

"Norman and Beanie have asked me to join them. I said I'd make some food, as it's so kind of them to include me. Beanie agreed and suggested we discuss the Christmas menu with Dotty now she's back."

"And you've booked your holiday to Morocco?"

"I have. For early January." Mick looked as guilty as a schoolboy. "It's all-inclusive, which means I don't have to pay extra for any food or drinks and, in the special offer, they waived the single supplement. The hotel has three swimming pools as well as a beach. And there are evening shows and trips out, although the trips cost extra."

"It would be nice to see some of the country while you're there," Keya suggested.

"That's what I thought, which is why I'm working on these Christmas orders so I can earn some extra money to pay for the outings."

"And there are a lot of orders," Keya observed, looking across at two tables filled with Christmas cakes of various sizes. Christmas puddings in plastic containers covered another table.

Millie joined Keya and said, "I'm going to miss all this."

"You're moving to Bristol with Ryan?"

"Yes, and sharing the rent means I can afford to apply for the apprenticeship the national supermarket chain is offering."

"I hope you get it."

"Thanks, and what about Maitri? Has she decided what she wants to do?"

"I'm not sure. Sis," Keya called, and when Maitri joined her and Millie, she said, "We haven't discussed your apprenticeship applications."

"No, but I sat down with Zivah yesterday and we decided..." She paused and grinned, "that I should apply for the one in London first, with the international hotel group, and if I'm not accepted for that, there are two or three courses and apprenticeships which remain open until Easter that I can apply for."

"I hope you get the one in London," Millie said.

"So do I. Can you imagine me serving afternoon tea to movie stars and royalty?" Maitri grinned and twirled away from them.

Millie looked at Keya and said, "But of course, if Maitri and I leave, you'll need more staff."

"Yes, but it's the nature of a business like this. And think who else I can help?"

Keya looked across at Mick as he delicately piped royal icing onto a Christmas cake under Monica's encouraging guidance. "I'm not going to worry about it until the New Year. Right now, I just want to enjoy the festive season."

CHAPTER FORTY-FIVE

"He's behind you!" cried Mick, and all the children in the pantomime audience at Cheltenham Theatre laughed as the oversized goose stepped to one side and round to the front of the stage while the dame, wearing a voluptuous blue and white checked dress, looked the other way.

Dotty had finally organised the trip for herself, her American friend Zach, Keya, and Sujin. Of their friends, only Mick had accepted the invitation to join them.

"This is such fun," Zach said, turning to Dotty.

"Have you ever seen a pantomime before?" Sujin asked him.

"Not a proper one like this. And I can't believe the theatre is full on New Year's Day. At home, everyone would be nursing hangovers," Zach replied.

"The same back in Glasgow. The Scots traditionally have two days off to recover from New Year's Eve," Sujin explained.

"A bit like Keya's café," Dotty smiled at her friend.

"Everyone worked so hard up to Christmas. They deserve a few extra days off," Keya protested. "And so do I, to be honest."

"You two have hardly taken a break with the amount of time you've spent at the inspector's house," Dotty commented. "By the way, what are you actually going to call it?"

"It's officially 53 London Road, but we thought we might call it Lefan Cottage, which is the original Welsh version of Evans," explained Keya.

"I think the inspector would like that," Dotty agreed.

"I must send him some photos," said Keya. "I wasn't sure about telling him the changes we were planning, but he was really enthusiastic about the idea. He said he'd considered it himself and told us where to find the plans he'd drawn up. That's why we were able to get a local builder to come in after Christmas and knock down the wall between the kitchen and dining room before he had to start back at a local housing site."

"Boo!" Mick shouted, leaning forward against the red velvet of the top of the balcony wall which ran round the upper circle.

"So that's enough about Sujin and me. What about you two?"

"I'm loving the Cotswolds and spending time with Dotty on her own, without a dead body," Zach smiled ruefully.

"I second that," said Sujin, grinning at Keya.

"I have to pop home for a couple of weeks to see my family, but I hope I can come back here afterward?" Zach regarded Dotty.

"I'd like that. Hopefully, we can complete your family treasure hunt and finish looking into your ancestry with the information you hope to collect when you're back in the States."

"And talking about family ancestry, I've persuaded Keya she should host a Burns Night supper at the café at the end of January," Sujin announced.

"With real haggis?" asked Zach eagerly.

"Vegetarian for me, but yes, real haggis. Sujin is organising people to read the poems, and he's asked the Celtic Twisters if they'll come and play."

"Do we have to dance?" asked Dotty uncertainly.

"It's called reeling, and yes, we have to learn how to do that," Keya replied. "Although, with the crime scene manager course starting this month, I'm not sure how I'll have the time to do everything. I might need your help organising the Burns Night Supper."

"Count me in," said Zach. "I'll even bring my kilt back from the States. It's going to be an eventful evening."

Thank you for reading *Hot Chocolate and A Festive Fatality*, the sixth and final book in The Waterwheel Café Mystery series.

But don't worry - Keya's adventures are far from over! You can follow the next case she is involved with in *Tartan, Treasures, and Trouble*, book 12 of The Dotty Sayers Antique Mystery series.

Tartan, Treasures and Trouble

New Year brings new dilemmas for Dotty. But when a Burns Night supper turns fatal, the stakes are higher than a Highland fling.

With Zach's family secrets unfolding and a killer on the loose, can Dotty solve the mystery before the echo of the bagpipes fades into silence?

Claim Your Copy of Tartan, Treasures and Trouble

Hour is Come

Would you like to read about Dotty's first case, and discover why she started solving murders and learning about antiques?

Find out and download *Hour is Come,* which is yours to keep when you sign up to my newsletter for updates. Click the QR Code below.

Earl Grey and Shallow Graves

Join Keya in her first book as she and her colleagues at Cirencester Police Station ensure justice is served, and the Cotswolds remain safe.

A 30-year-old skeleton. A missing girl. Can a community police officer read the tea leaves or will a deadly secret remain buried for ever?

Click the QR Code for more information.

For more information visit VictoriaTait.com

Made in the USA
Monee, IL
15 November 2024

70234974R00128